'Lauren?' he murmured, but if it was a question she had no idea of the answer.

Suddenly he tightened his grip again, wrapping his arms completely around her, and then he was rolling the two of them over.

He stared down at her for a moment that stretched into infinity and she could see the battle he was fighting with himself. She held her breath, trying to tell herself that she didn't care one way or another, then she saw his head angle towards her and she knew she'd lied.

Then his lips met hers in the briefest and most gentle of kisses, just a fleeting impression of sweetness and warmth. It was perfect, and yet almost as soon as it started it was over, and she was definitely disappointed when he lifted his head again. She'd wanted so much more.

Dear Reader

When I started planning these two books, I wanted to explore the effect that families—or lack of them—could have on us, so Lauren and Laurel were born.

Take a woman who's never really felt as if she belongs anywhere and put her together with a man who needs her to stay. There are bound to be sparks. Then throw in an accusation that the highly-recommended Nursing Sister he's just appointed might not be everything she seems…and yet, she's everything that he hasn't realised he wants.

Lauren is strong and self-sufficient because she's had to be. Then she meets Marc and needs to learn a whole new lesson…how good it can feel when someone really cares for you. And when it becomes more than caring…

Laurel's story *More Than a Gift* will be available in Medical Romance™ the month after next. I hope you enjoy finding out about each of them as much as I enjoyed the writing.

Josie

MORE THAN CARING

BY
JOSIE METCALFE

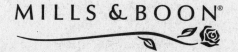
MILLS & BOON®

*All the characters in this book have no existence outside the imagination
of the author, and have no relation whatsoever to anyone bearing the
same name or names. They are not even distantly inspired by any
individual known or unknown to the author, and all the incidents are
pure invention.*

*First published in Great Britain 2002
Harlequin Mills & Boon Limited,
Eton House, 18-24 Paradise Road, Richmond, Surrey TW9 1SR*

© Josie Metcalfe 2002

ISBN 0 263 83094 2

*Set in Times Roman 10½ on 12 pt.
03-1002-47016*

*Printed and bound in Spain
by Litografia Rosés, S.A., Barcelona*

CHAPTER ONE

LAUREN stepped outside the hospital's side door, paused just long enough to hear the night safety lock catch, then closed her eyes in pleasure as she breathed in.

Even though she'd been in Edenthwaite ten days now, she was still amazed that the air was scented by the myriad things it had passed on its way from the distant fells. Perhaps in time she would become used to it, but after a busy first week on the staff at Denison Memorial, this was one of her newest pleasures.

She drew another draught deep into her lungs and let it out on a sigh. She really hoped that this would be the place that finally made her feel as if she could settle her roots permanently. She was so tired of feeling restless, especially as she didn't know what she was looking for.

Perhaps, surrounded by the wild beauty of such an unspoiled region of the country, she wouldn't feel the urge to see what lay over the next hill...unless she was wearing her new walking boots and doing the exploration just to familiarise herself with her new home.

'Only time will tell,' she murmured briskly as she set off towards the staff car park, then scowled at the darkness that enfolded her once she'd turned the first corner.

'The dratted man still hasn't done anything about

5

those lights,' she muttered, and made a mental note to beard the lion in his den. No matter what her personal feelings about Marc Fletcher, he was the hospital's chief administrator and, as such, ensuring staff safety was his responsibility.

It wasn't that the hospital was in a high-risk city— Edenthwaite couldn't have been more idyllic in the fading warmth of a September evening. Unfortunately, there were some facets of modern life that had permeated even this little corner of paradise, and one way to guard against them was to have safety lighting working once darkness fell.

'I told him about it the other day,' she grumbled under her breath, remembering the way the senior administrator had appeared in her department yet again. It was almost as though he didn't trust her to be able to do her job, although she knew for a fact that he'd checked every one of her references.

What was it about the man?

He knew that she was perfectly well qualified for the post, so it couldn't be that. And she hadn't had time to do or say anything to upset him.

'Mind you, I'm not sure how you'd tell if he *was* upset,' she added snidely, remembering the stony face he'd turned on her each time they'd encountered each other.

Not that he was bad-looking, by any means. His dark hair might be a little shorter than she preferred and the occasional silver strands at his temples made him look distinguished rather than older. His eyes were a strange smoky grey, almost as though the colour was a deliberate screen against anyone reading his thoughts.

As for his body, she was quite ashamed to admit

that she'd actually found her eyes following him as he'd stalked off down the corridor the other day. She'd been almost mesmerised by the lithe, ground-eating strides and the evidence of taut, compact muscles camouflaged by his impeccably pressed suit, and she wasn't someone prone to ogling men.

He certainly wasn't ogling her when he appeared in the ward, at least once every day. It was almost as if… 'As if he expects to find me pocketing the silver,' she finished on an exasperated laugh.

Well, if this continued she was going to have to confront him…ask him if he had some sort of problem with her. She was thoroughly enjoying her new post and if there was something she could do to remove the single fly in the ointment—a rather large fly going by the name of Mr Marcus Fletcher—then she just might have found that elusive niche she'd been searching for all her life.

In the meantime, she was going to have to mention the safety lighting again. One of the staff nurses had mentioned seeing someone loitering at one end of the staff car park, and as they hadn't been smoking, she'd known it hadn't been just a fugitive from Denison Memorial's strict no-smoking policy.

The thought of deliberately seeking out the openly disapproving man sent a shiver up her spine. There was just something about him that set all her nerves on edge; something she'd never encountered before and made her wary of him.

It wasn't that Marcus Fletcher was one of those enormous hulking brutes she'd grown accustomed to seeing when she'd started frequenting the gym a few years ago. He certainly didn't seem to be the type to waste his time building muscles for the sake of measuring the number of inches gained. He struck her as more the lean, predatory type—quietly fit and ready for anything that came his way. Or at least he might have been before he'd settled into his administrative job. There certainly wouldn't be much call for muscles when his day was spent wrestling with columns of figures.

Still, national statistics detailed a year-on-year increase in the number of attacks on all hospital employees, not just accident and emergency staff, a fact she'd seen for her own eyes in her last post at a busy city hospital. An injured friend had actually prompted her to offer her services to run several self-defence courses for her colleagues. Before she'd left, she'd had the satisfaction of knowing that at least two of her pupils had been able to use what they'd learned to ward off attackers.

A similar effort wouldn't go amiss at Denison Memorial.

Perhaps, she mused as she crossed the last open stretch before she got to her car, at the same time as she reminded her nemesis about the need to replace the lights as soon as they failed, she could make the same offer here—to run a basic course of self-defence for any female staff who were interested.

Yes, that's what she'd do as soon as she came in to work in the morning.

She was so busy thinking about her plans for the next day that she failed to follow one of her own basic rules—she had completely forgotten to be aware of what was going on around her.

The scuffling sound of furtive footsteps was only a few feet away from her when she suddenly became aware of them, almost too late to react.

'Laurel? Laurel Wainwright?' the shadowy figure demanded as he reached for one arm.

His grip was rough and bruising and for just a split second she was taken back to that nightmare time when she'd been sixteen and feeling so hopelessly alone and vulnerable.

Then Lauren's carefully honed instincts kicked in...literally. Shrugging off the memories that could still paralyse her with fear if she let them, she whirled into action.

It was easy enough, with a dozen years of practice behind her, to send her would-be assailant cartwheeling over her shoulder to land on the ground with a thud.

She barely had time to draw breath before she recognised the sound of more feet, running this time.

This man was bigger and stronger and she was careful to make sure that he didn't get a chance to grab hold of her before she flipped him over to join his partner in a heap.

'Dammit! What did you have to do *that* for?' the second assailant demanded angrily, already on his feet as quickly as a big cat and straightening up to his full height. His companion was taking far longer to drag himself up from his ignominious heap, but even *he* managed to get there in the end.

Lauren took a hasty step backwards, careful to remain out of reach. She certainly hadn't expected them to recover from her throws quite so quickly. The second one was almost as light on his feet as though he, too, was trained in martial arts, but she should have had time to get into the safety of her car before they both got their breath back.

As it was, the second one, the larger of the two,

was already taking a menacing step towards her and
she had to force herself to concentrate. It would do
her no good at all to notice that his shoulders seemed
much broader and his height much more impressive
now that he was prepared for her self-defence tactics.

She was just wondering whether she dared attempt
a kick manoeuvre on such a gravelly surface when
he spoke again.

'If you're thinking of drop-kicking me into next
week, don't bother,' he growled in a voice full of
disgust. 'I was only trying to help.'

'Help?' she exclaimed. 'Help who?'

'You, of course. I thought I saw someone following you when you left the hospital so I investigated.'

He'd gestured towards the way she'd come, turning just far enough for the light of a distant lamp to
catch his face, and she suddenly realised who he was.

'Mr Fletcher!' she gasped, horrified to realise that
she'd just flung the hospital's chief administrator
over her shoulder. He hadn't been very keen on her
appointment in the first place and this certainly
wouldn't make him any more pleased. 'I'm *so* sorry!
Did I hurt you?'

'Only my pride,' he said wryly, brushing the
gravel off the sleeve of his jacket. 'Who was your
friend?'

'My *friend*? He's no friend of…'

She suddenly remembered her first assailant and
whirled to discover that he'd taken advantage of her
preoccupation with her second opponent and disappeared into the surrounding darkness.

'Damn. Did you see which way he went?' she demanded.

'Why? I hope you're not thinking of chasing after him.'

'I should have kept my eye on him so he couldn't have got away in the first place,' she retorted. 'I *would* have done if you hadn't got in the way.'

'Well, excuse me for being concerned. I hope you're not waiting for me to apologise for coming to help,' he snapped, visibly affronted.

Lauren could almost feel sorry for him. Not many men could accept the fact that a woman didn't need them for protection. But, then, none of them would know about the situations she'd been in, where the only person she'd had to rely on had been herself.

'No, but if you'd done something about the broken lights when I told you about them, the whole situation could have been avoided,' she pointed out briskly. 'Perhaps you could manage an apology for that?'

'The broken lights were replaced within an hour of you reporting them to me,' he retorted stiffly. 'The safety of the staff while they're on Denison Memorial premises is my responsibility and I take my responsibilities very seriously.'

'Well, then, I suggest you check up on the quality of the lights,' she said as she turned towards her car, keys already in hand. 'Because they should certainly have lasted longer than a couple of days.'

Once in the car, she deliberately concentrated on the mundane task of fastening her seat belt so that she wouldn't have to look at him. She knew he was still standing there, just a few feet away, as though guarding her until she was ready to leave. She could feel those smoky grey eyes on her, almost as if they were touching her skin.

And all the while she was replaying his words inside her head.

I take my responsibilities very seriously.

There had been a definite undercurrent in his voice that had suddenly made her feel uneasy. She'd certainly lost her taste for standing there in the dark, sparring with the man.

She felt uncomfortable enough in his presence in broad daylight. With that critical gaze on her, all she wanted to do was leave the car park as soon as possible and make for the cosy sanctuary of her little cottage.

Lauren wasn't due to start her shift until half past seven the next morning, but seven o'clock saw her parking her trusty little car right under a light before she made her way inside.

In spite of her lingering embarrassment that she'd thrown him to the ground, she was still determined to approach the formidable hospital manager about running a self-defence class.

She'd planned to use her first break to visit his office, but just before she went in to change into her uniform she caught sight of him entering the lift on the way to his office.

'There's no time like the present,' she muttered as she opted to take the stairs, cross to feel the squadron of butterflies that suddenly took off in spectacular formation inside her stomach.

What was there to be nervous about? He'd either agree, or disagree. And with the suggestion coming from her, the odds were...

'Can I have a word, please?' she asked when his

deep voice bade her to enter, his secretary's desk still empty at this time of the morning.

'More lights to report?' One dark eyebrow shot up towards his ruthlessly neat hair.

'What?' She blinked, wondering for a moment what he was talking about. 'Oh, no. Not as far as I know. It's actually—'

'Someone had apparently been using the lights for target practice,' he announced grimly. 'Several had been smashed in the space of a single day.'

'Simple vandalism, then.' She sighed, completely sidetracked. 'As if the hospital didn't have enough calls on its budget, we now have to waste money on replacing safety lights on a daily basis.'

'It's nice to know *someone* appreciates that my balancing act isn't as easy as the media makes out,' he muttered, then threw her an unexpected grin. 'So, if it wasn't the lights, what *did* bring you into the dragon's lair?'

The startling change that single smile made to his face—the glint of amusement in those smoky grey eyes and the hint that the crinkles around them might have been put there partly by humour—took her breath away for a second. He really was an attractive man when you took away the weight of his responsibilities.

To cover up her momentary lack of attention Lauren cast a quick glance round the strictly functional room.

'Is that what this is? The dragon's lair?' she challenged lightly.

'You'd think so, from the fear and trepidation some people exhibit when they have to come here.' He leant back in his chair, the steel barrel of the pen he'd been using clasped between both hands as he rested his elbows on the arms.

His eyes only left hers for a second to drop in a swift sweep down her body and when a wash of heat followed it she felt almost as though she'd been just one pace too close to the fiery breath of the dragon.

'You, on the other hand, don't seem in the least bit intimidated,' he added thoughtfully, and she was relieved that he apparently hadn't recognised her reaction to him.

It was completely crazy. She had no more interest in him than he had in her. They were both hospital employees who, apart from his unofficial supervision, would have little cause to meet.

Even if her department were to need to requisition replacements for expensive equipment, the submission would be made on paper rather than in person. Yet, here she was, her eyes defensively fixed on the slender length of his fingers as he slid them back and forth on his pen, only too aware of the fact that his eyes were fixed on her face.

'Actually,' she said hurriedly, her face heating when she realised that he was still waiting for an answer, 'I wanted to ask how to go about arranging a series of self-defence classes.'

He gave a snort of laughter. 'I wouldn't have thought you needed any classes, seeing how you took care of two people all by yourself.' He pointedly rubbed one elbow with a grimace.

She laughed a little uncomfortably. 'Yes. Well, I'm sorry about that, but I wasn't asking about taking classes. I was actually proposing to teach them.'

'*You'd* teach them?' He seemed startled by the idea and her pride was stung. It wasn't only big burly men who could teach such things. Sometimes the fact that she was a slender female and well able to defend herself made her point to other women far more effectively.

'I've done them before, as I said on my CV,' she reminded him. 'At my last post, we were having increasing problems with hospital staff being attacked, especially in A and E. The first class started with a small group of female staff just from the accident department, and the word spread.'

He had a frown on his face and she was certain that he was going to turn the idea down. Whether that was because he disapproved of the proposal in principle or because of his continuing wariness about her, she didn't know.

Well, he might pour cold water on the suggestion this time, but that didn't mean that she wasn't going to bring it up again. She knew at first hand the benefits of learning self-defence and she would keep trying until he finally agreed to let her...

'I'll see what I can do about scheduling time in the physiotherapy department,' he announced, completely taking the wind out of her sails with his unexpected agreement.

'Oh, that's...great,' she managed, completely wrong-footed. She'd been so certain that she was going to have a fight on her hands.

'Unless I've got a meeting, I can usually manage to be free by six. Do you want me to organise it for after you've finished a shift, or would you rather I made it on one of your off-duty days?'

'Oh, but *you* don't have to be there,' she said hurriedly, suddenly nervous at the idea of having to put on a performance in front of eyes as keen as lasers.

'You'll need a body to use for your demonstrations,' he pointed out calmly, and her pulse tripped into overdrive.

He expected her to be able to concentrate while he grabbed her and held her close to that lean, muscular body? There might be a constant prickly animosity between the two of them but that didn't mean that her hormones couldn't recognise the fact that he was a good-looking man. In spite of the solemn expression he usually wore, he was so gorgeous that few women would want to fight him off.

Then her innate level-headedness kicked in and she brought her whirling emotions under control.

'You mean you're volunteering to get thrown around again? Wasn't one set of bruises enough for you?' she challenged.

He chuckled wryly and, much to her annoyance, her pulse kicked up another notch.

'At least this time I can make sure I won't be landing on concrete. In fact, I'll make sure the physiotherapy department has taken delivery of the new mats they ordered before I schedule the first class.'

Over the strident summons of one of the three telephones on his desk he promised to call her as soon as he had some dates for her, and suggested she have a think about how she wanted to publicise the classes.

On her way down to the ward to start her shift Lauren should have been thinking about the tasks awaiting her attention, or she should have set her concentration to deciding whether word of mouth would be a better advertisement than putting up posters. But all she could think about was Marc Fletcher's grin.

Well, it wasn't just his grin. It was the effect that smiling had on his whole face, from the sparkle it added to the smoky grey of his eyes to the lifting and lightening of the angle of his jaw and the gleam of strong teeth in a surprisingly sensual-looking mouth.

'Oh, good grief!' she muttered when she realised she was fixating on the man's teeth, for heaven's sake. 'He's the hospital manager, remember? He's got something against you that makes him turn up all the time to keep an eye on you, remember?'

In fact, now she thought about it, that was probably the reason why he'd suggested coming along to the classes, too. It wasn't that he wanted to offer his services as the willing victim so much as he wanted to see what she was getting up to.

Well, he wouldn't find anything amiss in one of her self-defence classes. She knew only too well how vital the information she would pass on could be— the difference between life and death, in some cases. There was no way she would do anything less than her best, no matter *who* was standing there supervising her.

In the meantime, there was a ward waiting for her to take over the reins, with the night staff champing at the bit to go home.

An hour later Lauren was beginning to wonder just how many more things were going to go wrong.

There had been a complete mix-up over the patients' meals, with dietary requirements completely ignored for some and meals being supplied for two ladies who were designated 'nil by mouth'.

'Surely you know that pre-operative patients

shouldn't be tucking into bacon and scrambled eggs?' she demanded of her hastily gathered staff once she'd sorted everything out. 'Just because the kitchen made a mess of things doesn't mean you switch your brains off. You know better than this.'

'I'm sorry, Sister,' muttered the hapless staff nurse, looking close to tears. 'It won't happen again, I promise.'

'See that it doesn't,' Lauren said sternly. 'Luckily, this time it won't make too much difference as Mrs Lisle hadn't eaten more than a couple of mouthfuls before she was stopped. I've warned Theatre that she'll have to be switched to the end of the list as a precaution.'

It was such an elementary mistake that she was quite concerned. Staff Nurse Roberts was usually very dependable. Such a potentially dangerous mistake was unlike her and would bear closer scrutiny.

'Next point on the agenda is the state of cleanliness, or rather the lack of it,' she said briskly. 'There are dust bunnies under some of those beds that are nearly old enough to talk and I spotted used paper hankies lying behind one of the curtains. In a postoperative ward that's a recipe for disaster. We don't want an environment where MRSA can flourish, so strict cleanliness, please.'

There were extra arrangements about transporting one patient up for X-rays and a rescheduling of physiotherapy for another, but Lauren was uncomfortably aware that her juniors were only too pleased to escape from her stern presence a few minutes later.

'Can't be helped,' she muttered under her breath as she accessed the computer records to correct the time of administering pre-med to the patient wrongly given her breakfast. 'I didn't enter nursing to win popularity contests, and the sooner they learn my ways, the sooner we'll get along with each other.'

Not that they were a bad bunch by any means. She'd found them very hard-working up to now, so perhaps this was just a minor glitch.

In the interim, she'd have to see if she could engineer a few minutes with Jackie Roberts. Perhaps over a cup of coffee she might loosen up enough to tell her what had brought on this unexpected lapse.

She nearly groaned when she saw how much to heart her nurses had taken her words. Over the next few hours there was almost a full-scale blitz on the ward with every surface attacked as though for a military inspection. What the cleaners didn't do, the nurses did, prompting the patients to joke that they were expecting to be next on the list for a good scrubbing.

With all that going on she should have had plenty to occupy her mind. Unfortunately that didn't stop her eyes straying towards the door every so often in expectation of seeing Marc Fletcher standing there with his habitual frown in evidence.

She was almost disappointed when the phone rang just before she was due to hand over at the end of her shift and she heard his voice instead. Had she actually been looking forward to seeing the man, even though she knew he was probably trying to find fault?

'Would Monday evening be good for your first session?' he asked briskly. 'That gives you four days to get the word around.'

Lauren's mind switched into high gear.

She still had a spare set of the notes she'd made

for the last course. It wouldn't be difficult to have them copied so each attendee could take a set home at the end of the session. That just left the publicising to organise.

'Monday works for me,' she agreed. 'And I wondered if it might be a good idea to start pretty low-key with the publicity this time. I thought I could put up notices in the female staff cloakrooms initially, to see what interest they stirred.'

'Sounds reasonable for a pilot scheme,' he said after a brief pause for thought. 'But put my phone as the contact number just to make sure you don't get any nuisance calls as a result.'

She'd been wondering how to get around that problem and was grateful for the suggestion but, 'Won't that tie up your line?' she worried.

'Rather mine than yours,' he said simply. 'People who need to get hold of me can always go through the switchboard and get my secretary if my direct line's busy. Anyway, it's better that way than leaving you open to the chance of an undesirable getting hold of your number.'

Lauren nodded, silently acknowledging the sense in his caution even though he couldn't see her. Part of her railed at the need for it, but she had to live with the reality of modern life. Before she had time to say anything, he was continuing inexorably.

'You'll want to give some guidelines about what clothes they'll need to wear, how many sessions and how long each session will last,' he listed without pausing for breath. 'If you drop off the outline with my secretary, she can photocopy it so you've got the right number to go around. Tomorrow morning, perhaps?'

He'd made it sound like a question but there was the unmistakable air of command in his tone that made her grin, glad that he couldn't see her response.

The hospital grapevine had suggested that Marc Fletcher had a military background and she could well believe it. He certainly liked to have everything organised and by the book.

'I'll do that,' she said, only just resisting the temptation to say Yes, sir!

Her mind was full of all the things she was going to have to do before she came to work the next morning—not least the fact that there was laundry waiting to be done and carpets needing a clean before she could settle down to design an eye-catching poster.

She wasn't so busy with her thoughts that she didn't notice that there was a full complement of safety lights this evening, but still she kept her eyes open. This time there were no unidentified people lurking in the shadows at the edge of the shrubbery, at least none that she could see.

She could chalk up her unfortunate experience yesterday to a random mugging that she'd foiled in spite of her inattention.

Still, there was a strange niggling doubt at the back of her mind. Something that she'd ignored, or a detail that had slipped her memory. There was something about the whole event…or non-event, as it had turned out…that was irritating her like a burr caught in clothing, if only she could remember what it was.

Unfortunately, the thing she remembered most clearly was the strangely electric sensation that had shot through her when she'd realised that the second man that she'd just deposited unceremoniously on the ground had been the punctilious Marc Fletcher.

Mixed in with the dismay at her *faux pas* was a wicked thrill that she'd actually caught the man by surprise and, big and strong as he was, flipped him base over apex.

She wished she had a photo of that. It was something that would have been able to make her smile on even the greyest of days. As it was, she was just going to have to rely on the memory.

CHAPTER TWO

MARC waited until he saw the taillights of Lauren's car disappear into the September dusk before he switched the light back on in his room and sat down behind his desk.

Wretched woman would probably cause a scene if she knew that he'd been looking out for her this evening, but he couldn't do anything else. At thirty-nine, the sense of responsibility had been part of him for far too many years for him to switch it off now.

If only he *could* switch it off, his life might be less stressful, but there would still be the guilt to keep him awake at night.

He sighed heavily, forcing himself to focus on the file spread open on his desk, then groaned again when he saw what it was.

In a larger hospital he wouldn't have been so intimately involved with so many of the different departments. Here, at Denison Memorial, he had a role to play in almost every aspect of the day-to-day running of things. That included being a member of the interview panel for the appointment of new members of staff, but he was guiltily aware *that* wasn't the reason why Lauren Scott's file was on his desk.

As she'd reminded him, there was documented evidence of the self-defence courses she'd run at her previous post. What she didn't know was that, in the course of checking her references, he'd also managed to find out about her involvement, almost to Olympic level, with several of the more strenuous forms of martial art.

He shook his head, bemused all over again. To look at her, so slender and elegant even in the loose-fitting tunic and trousers of her hospital uniform, you'd never know that her hands and feet could almost be classed as lethal weapons. Perhaps he should be counting himself fortunate that he had little more than a bruised elbow as a souvenir of their car park encounter.

He felt the wry smile edge over his face and knew that there was more than a hint of admiration in it. Her reaction to the perceived threat of his arrival on the scene had been so swift that he'd hardly had a chance to prepare himself for the impact.

He couldn't help admitting that this was a hidden side to her character that he found uncomfortably fascinating. He'd watched her at work on her ward and all he'd seen had been a gentle woman with a caring word or touch for anyone who needed it.

She was slightly taller than average but because she was slender he hadn't realised the fact until she'd faced him down in the car park. Then he'd had to notice that, in a pair of heels, her eyes would almost be on a level with his and her mouth...

'Her mouth would probably take a bite out of me, rather than kiss me,' he muttered, then was startled to feel a slow wash of heat spreading up over his face at the thought of those teeth sinking into his shoulder. And where had the thought of kissing her come from in the first place?

'Crazy!' he growled, slapping the file closed. 'Doubly crazy,' he added with a touch of bitterness that echoed around the unadorned walls of his office.

'She won't be staying long enough to start any kiss-ing. She *never* stays anywhere long enough. And anyway, you're not interested in starting any sort of relationship.'

He deliberately buried Lauren's file under the heap of paperwork still to be done before he went home.

Not that he was in any rush to leave the hospital. There certainly wasn't anything worth going home for. Just an empty cottage along a fairly isolated lane, one of a pair. He hadn't even had any neighbours until a week or ten days ago when someone had taken up residence while he'd been at work.

If he were the sociable sort he could have gone round with a welcoming bottle of wine or something. As it was, he was grateful that whoever was renting the property seemed to lead just as busy a life as he did and was quietly content to keep himself to him-self. The last thing he needed was some happy couple living right under his nose, reminding him of every-thing that was missing in his own life. Thank good-ness the cottage was too small to accommodate a family with children.

Not that he begrudged others their happiness. He'd had it all once, until his own selfishness had put it in danger. He'd had to come to terms with the fact that duty and responsibility were going to fill his life from now on.

'And paperwork,' he said with a baleful glare, sud-denly loathing the fact that his job involved so little activity. Once upon a time... 'No. It's over. Finished!' he said fiercely. 'I can take care of people just as effectively this way—by making sure that their medical services are running properly—as I ever could by running around, playing the hero.'

He forced himself to concentrate on the latest fore-cast figures for the hospital wages but still couldn't stop the sudden shiver of awareness that snaked up his spine at the thought of Lauren's self-defence class. She was intending that the first sessions were just going to be run for interested female staff and was probably hoping that, in spite of his offer to help with her demonstrations, he would be happy to sit at the back as an observer.

What she didn't know was that he had every in-tention of being an active member of those classes. What *he* didn't know was whether that decision was based on the desire to make sure that the lessons were thorough and accurate, or whether it had any-thing to do with the growing need to see if Lauren's slender body was every bit as lithe and strong as he remembered.

'Damn. I'm going to be late!' Lauren muttered with a quick glance at her watch. She hastened her steps past the X-ray department, wondering why some days turned out like that.

She should have had plenty of time to get to the physiotherapy department and give her notes a final read through before the first brave souls arrived. Now she'd be lucky to get there before it was time for the class to start.

'Ah! Here she is!' called a male voice as she pushed the doors open, and she had to deliberately tamp down the swift surge of pleasure that Marc's husky voice set off.

Then she saw him and almost forgot how to breathe.

He looked good in the business suits he wore to

work each day, but in the softly draping fabric of a tracksuit she could see just how well the formal clothing camouflaged the muscles beneath. And to see him lounging easily against the wall with his arms folded across an impressively broad chest…

It was a real physical effort to drag her eyes away and acknowledge the half-dozen assorted members of staff waiting for her.

'Sorry to be late but I got delayed on the ward,' she said in a strangely breathless voice.

'You don't need to apologise to *us*. We know it goes with the territory,' groaned a staff nurse she vaguely recognised from the accident and emergency department. It was amazing the difference a slim-fitting pair of jeans made when she was accustomed to seeing the young woman in baggy cotton theatre greens.

'It doesn't help when staff numbers are down either,' said another with a dark look in Marc's direction.

'You don't need to tell me,' he said, his hands held up in surrender as he shouldered himself away from the wall to join the group. 'Most nurses are working the equivalent of one and a half jobs but aren't being paid a fair rate for one. That's why recruitment is so difficult.'

'Well, love of the job won't pay the grocery bills,' said another voice, and Lauren realised her class was in danger of being hijacked by the perennial nursing complaint.

'So, does anyone here want to learn how to defend themselves against people desperate to mug them for their lavish salary?' she joked, and heard the mixture of groans and chuckles she was looking for. 'If you'd like to come over and perch yourselves on these benches, we'll start with a few basics.'

'This reminds me of being in gym classes at school,' said Sam, the youngest member of the group, with a giggle as they settled in a row on the low wooden bench.

'OK, now, I'll start with a general introduction. For those who don't know me, I'm Lauren Scott, a recent recruit to Denison Memorial. Before I came here I worked in a big inner city hospital in a rather rough part of an industrial town. It was bad enough having to cope with so many victims of physical violence but when some of them were our own staff, I wanted to see if I could do something about it.'

She paused a moment to draw breath, needing to subdue the ache of memories of a friend she would never see again, knifed right outside the hospital by an assailant trying to snatch her bag to support a drug habit. If she had her way, none of these women would end up victims. That was what she should concentrate on.

'At school I was into sport and, like a lot of women, I enjoyed pitching myself against the boys in my class.' There was another chuckle and some shared glances that told her she hadn't been the only one. 'Unfortunately, as we moved up the school, the boys got bigger and stronger, especially in their upper bodies, and when I realised that I was going to have to learn to use guile to beat them, I turned to martial arts.' It wasn't the whole story by a long chalk, but it was enough to get their attention.

'You mean judo? That sort of thing?' Sam asked eagerly. 'There have been several films recently with women doing that.'

'Judo and Tae Kwon Do,' Lauren said with a nod. 'It came in very useful when the body-builders tried to get a little more friendly than I wanted, but it wasn't until a couple of years ago that I realised how few women know how to defend themselves against the threat of random violence.'

'But if it's random, you can't be prepared against it, can you?' objected one of her older pupils, a senior nurse from the A and E department. 'It *must* be different if you're waiting for a bell to go at the start and finish of a bout in a competition.'

In spite of the fact that she'd carefully positioned herself to keep him out of her direct line of sight, Lauren caught a glimpse of Marc's expression and was suddenly gratified to see that he was every bit as interested in what she had to say as the rest.

She dragged her eyes away and forced herself to gather her thoughts.

'In one way, you're absolutely right. You can never know when violence might explode out of no-where. But you can be prepared, especially if you learn to take sensible precautions on a daily basis.'

Getting into her stride, she started off with what was for her the number one rule.

'The best way to get out of a difficult situation isn't becoming an expert at martial arts, it's running,' she announced baldly, and watched them blink.

'You mean, go to keep-fit classes, or take up jogging?' Marc asked with a frown. It obviously wasn't what he'd expected. He looked almost as though she'd disappointed him.

'Not necessarily, although we could probably all do with a bit of extra exercise if only we had the time and energy,' Lauren said. 'No, what I actually mean is, if you're attacked, the best thing you can do is to run away—even if your attacker has grabbed your handbag. It's never worth being injured or even losing your life over a bag full of odds and ends.'

Lauren reached for the shoulder-bag she'd deposited with her notes and demonstrated how to carry it tucked tightly under her arm with the long handles folded well out of reach.

'Most attacks on lone women happen at night, so it's important that you're aware of any dangerous places on your journey—badly lit short cuts, for example—and that you find a safer way to go.'

She had their attention now but, strangely, she was most aware of a certain pair of smoky grey eyes following her every word.

'I've prepared a set of notes that you can each take home with you at the end of the session, just to remind you of the points that we'll go through in each class.'

She handed out the notes and waited a moment till they settled down again then began working her way through the list of basic safety strategies for women travelling alone.

It turned into a lively discussion…much to Marc's surprise, if she was reading his expression correctly.

Had he expected her just to stand in front of them and deliver a dry lecture? she wondered crossly. Just wait until she started teaching them some of the really physical stuff. She'd prove to him that she was just as good at this as she was at her nursing job.

'As you can see, self-defence has some similarities with medicine,' she pointed out. 'Much of the prevention side is just common sense.'

'Like parking in well-lit areas,' Marc said, a meaningful glint in his eye just for Lauren.

'Which brings us back to the aspect of planning ahead,' she hastily added, hoping the sudden wash of heat she could feel in her face wasn't showing as a blush. 'If you're parking a car during the day, don't forget to check that it's still going to be a safe position to come back to at the end of your shift when it's dark.'

'There was one of those programmes on the television that gave out advice like this and they said you should have your keys in your hand when you go out to your car,' Sam offered.

Lauren was delighted that the youngest member of the group had so much to contribute. She was such a bubbly personality that she would be an excellent person to spread the word about the classes.

'Do the rest of you know why?' Lauren asked, opening the question up to the whole group. 'Can you suggest any reasons why it would be a good idea to carry your keys on the way to your car?'

'You wouldn't have to stand there for ages trying to fish the darned things out of the bottom of your bag,' groaned one.

'You'd have them in your hand to use as a weapon,' suggested her bloodthirstier neighbour.

'It's down to that ''be prepared, look prepared'' thing again, isn't it?' said a third. 'You won't look like a dithery potential victim.'

'Good,' Lauren said, trying to block out the approving nod she caught from Marc. She didn't need it to tell her that this was probably the most receptive group she'd had so far. Or was that just her heightened perception because of the presence of her largely silent observer?

'Now, let's take it a step further. You've unlocked the car. What do you do next?'

'Get in quickly and lock the door?' suggested one with a smile.

Lauren had turned towards her as she'd spoken, so she saw Marc silently reach out towards the speaker in front of him.

'And what if you've just locked yourself in the car with a stalker?' he growled menacingly as he placed his hands around her neck.

The young nurse's shriek was almost enough to curdle the blood. It was certainly enough to drive the point home.

'As Mr Fletcher has just kindly demonstrated,' Lauren said to a slightly nervous chorus of chuckles, 'you should always look in the back of the car before you get in, to make sure you haven't picked up any unwanted passengers. And do it *every* time you leave the car, even if it's been parked on a brightly lit forecourt while you filled up with petrol. To be really safe, lock the car when you go to pay for the fuel, and take your handbag with you.'

'It's all such obvious stuff, isn't it?' groaned her oldest pupil, Marion. 'So simple that we should be doing it on an everyday basis without even thinking about it.'

'If it's any consolation, it doesn't take long before it actually *does* become routine,' Lauren promised. 'By the time you finish the course you'll find that it's become automatic to plan an outing with the safety factor as an integral part of it. You'll no more think about setting off without making arrangements for your return than you'd go on a journey without letting someone know where you're going and what time you expect to arrive back. You're just planning to stay safe—and stay alive—without letting fear take over and rule you. After all, it'll probably never happen, especially if you take precautions.'

'What about at home? Do we need to turn our houses into fortresses?' Marion asked.

'Only if the Queen's in the habit of lending you the crown jewels on a regular basis,' Lauren teased. 'Most people need do nothing more than fit good locks and a safety chain and make sure they use them.'

Lauren invited questions but they all seemed perfectly happy with the basics they'd covered so far. A quick glance at her watch told her that they still had plenty of the allotted time left but she didn't know whether the group would have had enough for one session and decided to leave the decision up to them.

'Well, ladies…and gentleman,' she added with a tilt of her head towards Marc, 'that's the end of the first part—the mainly theoretical side concerned with trying to avoid getting into dangerous situations. Have you had enough to take in for one day, or do you want to continue?'

'Is this the bit where we learn how to throw giants around like matchsticks?' her youngest pupil demanded with relish. 'Like that kung fu stuff they do in films?'

'And leap tall buildings in a single bound? Not exactly, Sam,' Lauren said with a grin. 'If you want to learn martial arts you'll have to find classes where they can teach you from scratch. Here, you're just learning the basics to help you get out of dangerous situations. And remember, the most important one is to run.'

'*Run?*' her young pupil said dismissively. 'Running away's cowardly. I'd rather wipe the floor with the so-and-so who tries to attack me.'

Lauren saw the frown beginning to darken Marc's face and had a feeling that he was tempted to break in. She was glad when he resisted the urge.

She confronted the problem head on, hoping to inject a touch of humour to get it across.

'OK, Sam, I know that we're always taught that it's cowardly to run away from our problems,' she agreed. 'And I'd be the first to admit that it can give you a buzz when you manage to throw a much bigger opponent…' She paused just long enough for another, more wicked grin, telling herself that it wasn't being aimed at Marc. 'But I doubt the buzz would last very long when you realised what damage he'd done to your face with the knife he was carrying in his other hand. Or what about the broken jaw or the shattered eye socket when your attempts failed on the first try and you only succeeded in making him angry?'

Several members of the class pulled faces and Lauren could see from the thoughtful expression on Sam's face that she might have succeeded in her aim.

'At this moment, we're just interested in defensive manoeuvres rather than offensive ones. But if you're feeling particularly bloodthirsty there's nothing to say that you couldn't have all the fun you need, learning to throw people around in classes. Now, who's going to be my guinea pig while I do some basic demonstrations?'

Lauren was expecting Sam to be the keenest but before the young woman even had a chance to offer, Marc was on his feet and making his way to the front of the group.

'It would make more sense if I volunteered,' he

said firmly, the direct expression in those smoky grey eyes almost daring her to object. 'Then all the others get an equal chance to see what's going on.'

He was right, of course, but just the thought of being in any sort of close contact with the man was enough to have her pulse throbbing at twice its usual rate.

'Well, yes, of course,' she muttered, startled to realise that there was more than a little anticipation mixed in with the apprehension. 'Good idea.'

'So,' he said as he pushed his sleeves up to reveal surprisingly muscular forearms shaded with dark hair, 'what do you want me to do?'

'Grab me...or rather, grab my clothing,' she directed, then prayed that she'd manage to fight the blush working its way up from her throat. 'I want to demonstrate how to break your hold.'

It didn't take long to demonstrate several ways to break an attacker's hold but Lauren was glad when it was time for each member of the class to take a turn to be victim and aggressor. At least with Marc sharing the supervision she had a chance to calm down.

It shouldn't be like this, she told herself sternly. He was just a colleague, and a rather disapproving one at that. He certainly wasn't someone who should be sending her hormones into orbit when all he was doing was grabbing hold of a handful of her clothing.

'Now, grab my hair,' she directed, trying to adopt an air of briskness as she demonstrated several ways of breaking his hold while losing as little hair as possible in the process. 'And don't forget, as soon as you've broken free, run before he's had a chance to work out how you got away.'

Once again, Marc assisted as each of the members

of the class practised the simple manoeuvres that would startle an attacker into releasing his hold.

It was just by chance that Lauren caught sight of the clock on the wall and realised that they'd overrun their allotted time.

She could almost have predicted the groans that went up when she called an end to the session. All of them were obviously taking everything seriously, but that didn't mean that they weren't prepared to have fun while they were learning. Especially if it came at Marc's expense, it seemed.

'If you're going to start teaching them how to throw me around, I don't think I'll come next time,' he groaned theatrically as they made their farewells. The others laughed sympathetically and promised to dump him gently if he was brave enough to turn up for the next instalment.

Lauren was surprised at the sudden stab of disappointment his announcement caused, then cross with herself for being disappointed.

She hadn't expected him to turn up in the first place and when he had, she hadn't expected that he would be so helpful, not after the way he'd been keeping such an eagle eye on her in the ward.

She also hadn't expected to find herself responding to him as anything other than the man intent on watching and waiting for her to make a disastrous error of some sort. She certainly didn't want to see him as an attractive man who set her blood racing.

'Thank you for your help,' she said politely as he waited beside the door to switch the light off behind them.

'You're welcome. I actually enjoyed it.'

Lauren couldn't help chuckling. 'In a masochistic way?'

'Sounds like it, doesn't it?' He gave one of those grins guaranteed to set a firecracker under any woman's libido. 'I actually meant the whole thing. You're good at putting the stuff across so they take it in.'

'I had a good teacher,' she said briefly, allowing herself a fleeting memory of the indefatigable woman who had made it her life's mission to teach self-defence after she'd lost her only daughter in an attack.

They'd reached her car, sitting safely under the blue-white glow of the safety light. As she turned to say goodnight she was suddenly aware of a strange reluctance for the evening to end. Not that she had any reason to prolong her farewell. Marc was far too busy even to take time out to attend her class this evening, let alone walk her out to her car.

'Lauren, you haven't remembered anything more about the other night, have you?' he demanded, much to her surprise. She'd actually managed to put the whole incident to the back of her mind.

'Remembered anything more?' she repeated, puzzled. 'Like what? I barely saw the man because it was so dark, remember?'

'So you wouldn't recognise him if you saw him again?'

'Not if he were standing in front of me right this minute,' she confirmed honestly.

'Well, did he say anything? Make any threats? Did he have a particular regional accent, for example?'

'I honestly can't remember…' she began, only to pause as that niggling impression rose up from its hiding place in the back of her mind. 'Wait a minute… There was something…'

He started to speak but she put up her hand to stop

him, not wanting anything to interfere with her concentration. There had definitely been something odd
about the encounter...something that had stuck like
a burr in a totally inaccessible place...

'He called out to me,' she said aloud as she ran
through the events, like replaying a video in her
mind. 'I'd broken my own rules because until he
spoke I hadn't even realised that he was there. Then
he grabbed me...'

'And you sent him neatly over you to land in a
heap,' Marc finished for her with an unexpected edge
of satisfaction in his voice. 'I saw that part, but do
you remember what his voice sounded like? Or what
he said?'

'My name. No! *That* was it! It *wasn't* my name,
but just for a moment I thought it was, so I was a
bit slow on the uptake.'

'So, what *did* he say?'

'He called me Laura...no, *Laurel* something. I can't
remember exactly.' Lauren resorted to the trick she
used with crossword puzzles of running through the
alphabet in her mind. She'd almost reached the end
when she exclaimed, 'Wright! No, that's still not
quite... Something-Wright... Arkwright? Wainwright?
Yes! That's it. He called me Laurel Wainwright.'

'And you've no idea why?'

'None at all. I've never heard the name before.'

'And it's not as if you're from the area, so he
couldn't have recognised you and just forgotten your
name,' Marc mused.

'Oh, well. It's probably destined to remain one of
life's great mysteries,' Lauren quipped. 'Along with
what happened to my other pair of walking socks

when I did the laundry yesterday. I could have sworn I put both pairs in, but only one pair came out.'

'Hmm. They can't have gone to the Planet of Lost Socks, then. They only accept them if they arrive one at a time,' Marc retorted with a straight face, then spoilt it by laughing at her expression.

Lauren couldn't help joining in. The last person from whom she'd have expected such whimsical nonsense was super-efficient, perennially serious Marc Fletcher, but with just that one sentence he'd revealed another, deeply hidden facet.

Suddenly, she knew she was in trouble; knew it was time she said a swift goodbye and made her way as far away from the man as quickly as she could.

It had been easy to resist his physical attraction…with a minor lapse or two while she'd watched that gorgeous body striding away down yet another corridor. All the while he was being so suspicious and grouchy her emotions were in no danger.

Unfortunately, the Marc Fletcher she'd seen this evening was another matter altogether—generous with his time, sharply intelligent, and with a surprising sense of the absurd.

This was a man who could easily chip away at the self-sufficiency that had become so much a part of her over the last decade or so.

CHAPTER THREE

'LAUREN? It's Marc Fletcher,' said the voice on the other end of the phone.

Her knees gave a very unseemly wobble but Lauren firmly refused to admit that *that* was the reason why she perched swiftly on the corner of the desk. She was a responsible ward sister after all, not a teenager with a crush on the nearest good-looking boy.

Nor was Marc Fletcher a boy, not with those broad shoulders and muscular legs, to say nothing of the age and experience he couldn't hide no matter how enigmatic the expression in those smoky grey eyes.

And the fact that she'd hardly seen him in nearly a week had nothing to do with her reaction either. She'd told herself that he must have been too busy to check up on her, or perhaps she'd somehow convinced him that she was no threat to his precious hospital. She'd also told herself that she should be glad that he wasn't breathing down her neck all the time. What she *couldn't* tell herself was that she'd been relieved not to see him.

'How can I help you?' she returned brightly, determined that he shouldn't have a hint of the turmoil just the sound of his voice engendered in her these days.

'I've got my bed manager's hat on at the moment, so this call's just by way of a rather late warning that I'm sending you another patient. The ambulance set off about an hour ago so she should be with you fairly shortly.'

She could hear something in his tone that told her there was something a bit different about this admission, then marvelled at the flight of fancy. As if she could possibly know the man well enough to read such things into his voice…and over the phone, no less.

'Actually,' he continued after a thoughtful pause, 'there's a bit of a tale behind her condition, but I'll leave it to her to tell you.'

Lauren was torn between shock that she had been right about his tone of voice and curiosity at the mystery.

'You're not going to tell me any more, are you?' she accused. 'You're just going to leave me dangling until she gets here.'

'Well, I can tell you that she's been in your old city hospital for nearly a month and needs another week or ten days of your gentle ministrations before she'll be ready to go home again. Apart from that, I'll just tell you that she's either been remarkably unlucky or extremely lucky. I'll leave it to you to decide when you've spoken to her.'

With that, he hung up, leaving Lauren spluttering.

At the end, there, she'd been sure there had been an almost playful tone to his voice and it certainly wasn't like the formidable man she'd first met to taunt her with a 'wait and see' situation.

Now she could hardly wait for the woman to arrive. She was also going to have to find some way to turn the tables on him, unless…

She grinned when she remembered what day it was. Tonight she was due to teach the second self-defence class, and if Marc fulfilled his intention of providing her with a demonstration opponent, she was going to be able to do more than turn the tables on him. She might actually be able to turn his whole world upside down.

She grinned at the image of Marc lying in a crumpled heap at her feet, the victim of yet another crime-busting manoeuvre.

'Mrs Roker's here, Sister,' said a voice behind her, and she suddenly realised that she was still standing there with the telephone clutched in her hand and an inane grin on her face. She hadn't even had time to run a critical eye over the bed that her new charge was to occupy to make sure that everything was exactly the way it should be.

'Good. I'm coming,' she said hastily, cradling the phone and smoothing her hands over her uniform before she hurried out into the ward.

'Please, Sister, call me Cissy,' her new patient requested when they'd finally got her settled into her bed.

'If that's what you'd prefer,' Lauren agreed as she retrieved the thick file of notes that had arrived with her latest charge. 'It looks as if by the time I've read all this lot I'll know your complete life's history.'

'Oh, no, Sister,' Cissy exclaimed. 'That's just the last couple of months. The rest of my life would probably fit on a single sheet of paper, and that includes having four children.'

'Wow.' Lauren blinked when she had her first inkling of what Marc had been hinting at. 'How about if you give me the edited highlights as an introduction?'

'Well, Sister, I think you'd better make yourself

comfortable. This is more of a saga than a two-minute short story.'

Lauren chuckled as she perched one hip on the edge of the bed, careful not to move the cage keeping the weight of the bedclothes away from Cissy's injured leg.

'It all started when I went in to have my blood pressure checked just after my seventieth birthday,' she began. 'Well, my doctor—not one of the ones at Denison Memorial, by the way; we live a little further afield—he said it was fine and did I have any problems he could help me with? I said I was fit as a fiddle apart from the nasty scrape on my shin from where I'd caught it when I walked into the edge of the coffee-table. He took a quick look at it and suggested I went straight along to the practice nurse to have it cleaned up and a protective dressing put on it.'

Lauren suddenly noticed that the room seemed strangely quiet. A quick glance around told her that almost every person in the room had tuned into the tale and was waiting with bated breath for Cissy to continue.

'Well,' Cissy went on, her softly lined face animated, 'she cleaned it up and put some stuff on it. Then, because my skin's a bit thin, she put a bandage on instead of a sticky plaster and told me to come back in three days to have the dressing changed.'

Apparently blithely unaware of her audience, she drew a quick breath and continued. 'It was a different nurse the next time and when she took the bandage off she said it was an awful waste of dressings for such a little scrape. I tried to tell her what the first nurse had said about my skin but she got all huffy.'

Cissy stuck her nose in the air and put on an affected voice. '"I *do* know what I'm doing, Mrs Roker. I'm a fully qualified nurse, you know."'

Lauren couldn't help joining in the round of chuckles. The woman was evidently a wicked mimic as well as a natural storyteller.

'Anyway, when she put the sticky plaster on, I had to tell her that she'd stretched it too tight and it was pulling the skin. Well, she took hold of the corner and whipped it up—the way you nurses often do to get it over and done with—and she took off a chunk of skin with it.'

This time it was a chorus of sympathetic murmurs and winces and Lauren noticed that Cissy had started playing to the gallery.

'She stuck it straight back down again, pretending that she hadn't realised what she'd done, and told me to come back in four days, but by that time it was pretty sore.'

Lauren guessed that *that* was probably an understatement. If this was the first real medical problem she'd undergone in her life, Cissy obviously wasn't one to complain lightly.

'It was the first nurse again, thank goodness, and she was cross when she saw the plaster, especially when I told her I'd explained about the bandage to the other nurse. Then, when she took it off and saw the mess underneath, she had to ask the doctor to come in—not my own doctor because he was away on holiday by then.'

'So, how was the graze you'd needed the dressing on in the first place? Was it healing while all this was going on or had it got worse, too?' Lauren asked.

'It was nearly gone, dear,' Cissy said. 'It was the

place where that other nurse had pulled the skin off that had flared up, so the doctor gave me some antibiotics and told me to come back in three days to have the dressings changed again. Only I couldn't wait three days because the pain got so bad and my leg kept swelling up more and more.'

'You saw your own doctor again?' Lauren was suddenly aware just how long this tale might go on for if she didn't give it a gentle nudge along.

'No, it was the locum standing in for my own doctor while he was away on holiday. He took one look and told me I needed to go to the hospital straight away. Not Denison either, but the big one in the city.'

Bearing in mind that this had all happened nearly a month ago, Lauren was almost dreading what would come next. It must have been a serious problem to have kept her in hospital all this time.

'Well, when I got to the hospital they poked and prodded and took blood and X-rays and then a young man asked me to sign a piece of paper. ''What's that for?'' I asked. ''For your amputation tomorrow morning,'' he said as calm as you like. ''We're going to be cutting your leg off because you've got gangrene.'' And he never batted an eyelid.'

This time it was gasps of horror that went round the room. Lauren had heard similar stories in the ten years since she'd started her training but the word 'gangrene' still gave her the shivers.

'''Then I'm not going to sign it,'' I said,' Cissy continued fiercely, still recounting the conversation, '''because I'm not going to let you cut my leg off.'' And I told him he'd better sort that gangrene out, or else!'

Lauren was almost itching to read the case notes now. It would be very interesting to learn how Cissy had escaped death if her circulation had been spreading the deadly gangrene through her body.

'Well, I was in Intensive Care for over two weeks but I've still got my leg,' Cissy announced proudly, leaning forward just far enough to pat the blanket-covered tunnel protecting the precious limb. 'Now all I need is for you to help me get steady on my feet again so I can go home.'

'We'll certainly be doing our best,' Lauren promised, and when she caught sight of a trolley out of the corner of her eye, continued, 'How about starting off your recovery with a nice cup of tea?'

'Lovely, dear.' Cissy smiled beatifically. 'Milk but no sugar—I'm sweet enough without it!'

'Makes interesting reading, doesn't it?' said a familiar voice behind her as Lauren neared the end of Cissy Roker's thick file of notes.

'Marc!' she exclaimed, then wondered if her smile had been too broad to welcome a visiting colleague. In spite of her age, she wasn't accustomed to dealing with such unruly emotions. Initially, she'd decided to concentrate her attention on her career but even when she'd realised that her life could be lonely, the fact that she'd moved hospitals so often in search of that elusive *something* missing in her life meant she hadn't had time to form close relationships.

If she were truthful, the effect this man had on her was a little frightening in its intensity, and that wouldn't do, especially when there was absolutely no evidence that she was affecting him the same way. If there was any chance that she was going to settle

permanently in Edenthwaite, she was going to have
to get her head together and the sooner the better.

In the meantime, her heart might be thumping out
of all proportion but there was no reason to let him
know that he had such an effect on her.

'Yes, it's very interesting reading,' she agreed,
hastily returning her gaze to the paperwork with the
fervent hope that she hadn't been gazing up at him
with a moonstruck expression on her face. 'And I
saw what you meant about her luck. She must be one
of the few people to be grateful that the circulation
in her leg had all but shut down.'

'It certainly meant that the gangrene hadn't spread
so far,' he agreed, showing that he obviously knew
enough to realise that her condition could have been
fatal.

Lauren found she wasn't surprised. After all, in
his job he must hear medical terms bandied about all
the time. He was obviously intelligent enough to put
two and two together. 'It was just a damned shame
that nurse didn't have her wits about her when she
was replacing that original dressing.'

'Or the humility to admit she'd got it wrong when
she tore Cissy's skin, and treated it properly straight
away, rather than just sticking the plaster over it
again and pretending it hadn't happened,' Lauren
added with a frown.

'I gather you've been treated to the full story. I
only had the condensed version passed on by her
consultant, and that was bad enough.'

'Well, she certainly seems to have used the situation to prove that determination can move moun-
tains. She's still alive and she's still got both legs
and she's absolutely itching to get going again.

Apparently, she makes and decorates cakes for friends and family—birthdays and anniversaries and so on. She's determined she's not going to let anybody down this Christmas in spite of the fact that she was staring death in the face just three weeks ago.' She threw Marc a quick smile but was careful not to meet his eyes. 'I really admire the way some people just seem to be able to shrug off disasters and carry on regardless.'

He was silent for so long that eventually Lauren couldn't help looking up at him, only to catch a glimpse of shadows left by a deep sorrow. Then he blinked and the expression was gone so quickly that she almost doubted that she'd seen it.

Except, now that she thought about it, there was a lingering air of melancholy about the man and the impression that he was suppressing some deep feelings seemed to surround him with an almost electric aura.

She had thought him a very calm, controlled man when she'd first met him, one liable to make decisions that became set in stone. Now she wondered just how wrong she'd been about his nature. Were there strong emotions hidden under that faultlessly pressed shirt and smart grey business suit?

His pager gave a sudden chirrup and she knew she'd seen the last of him…at least until her class tonight.

She was surprised when, instead of hurrying out of the little office, he paused at the door.

For a moment it looked as though he might still depart without a word, then, 'Perhaps some people are more resilient than others,' he murmured quietly. 'Or perhaps they aren't hampered by guilt.'

*   *   *

Lauren was still pondering those perturbing words when she welcomed the first arrivals in the physiotherapy department that night.

'Are we going to get physical tonight?' demanded Sam as she bounced in, wearing a shiny stretch outfit in cerise and lime green that would have looked far more in keeping with a trendy gym than a hospital physiotherapy department.

Rather than Lauren's slender shape, Sam had the toned curvaceous figure that would have any man salivating on sight. Perhaps it was a good thing that she was learning self-defence if that was the sort of thing the young woman regularly wore in public.

'I'll be teaching you a few more manoeuvres to practise,' Lauren confirmed. 'But as you'll be working with each other, you won't actually be doing any throws. We don't want anyone getting hurt.'

The rest of the group arrived then, all apparently keen to begin even though the class was taking place at the end of a busy day. Lauren took it as a compliment to her teaching that she hadn't lost a single member of the original group—except for Marc, that was.

After the events of that afternoon she'd been certain he'd be here and it was a disappointment. He'd seemed genuinely interested in Mrs Finch and she'd convinced herself that he'd probably wanted to find out how she was.

They'd been in the middle of a crisis when she'd heard him enter the ward.

'I'll be with you in a moment, if you'd like to wait in my office,' she'd said calmly, and had almost forgotten he'd been there as she'd struggled to do everything at once without frightening the elderly woman.

There must have been something in her voice that had made Marc take a closer look at the woman in the bed.

'Heart attack?' he demanded quietly, obviously having read the signs of her patient's distress.

'Angina attack,' Lauren corrected, struggling one-handed with slippery packaging. 'I've given her one of her tablets but I need—'

Before she could say anything further he'd taken the package from her, stripped the oxygen mask out of it and connected it to the piped oxygen as efficiently as if it was something he did every day.

'Thank you,' she said, throwing him a distracted smile as she settled the mask over the elderly woman's face.

To her surprise, far from stepping back and letting her continue, he reached for Mrs Finch's wrist, obviously intent on monitoring her pulse.

'Still not good,' he muttered. 'How long ago did you give her the tablet?'

Before she could think to comment on his apparent expertise or give him an answer, Norman Castle came hurrying in, called up from the GP practice housed in the east wing of Denison Memorial.

'Amelia, my dear, don't tell me you've been getting yourself all upset over those wretched boys of yours,' he said, giving Lauren a nod as he took her place at the side of the bed, his hand now holding the fragile wrist.

'What on earth had she been doing to bring that on?' Marc asked when the two of them retired to the foot of the bed.

'She's a bit forgetful and couldn't remember when her sons last visited her. She'd convinced herself they must be ill and was trying to get dressed to go home to them.' She gave a frustrated huff. 'If I had more nurses on the ward we might have had a chance to see how worked up she was getting before it got this far.'

She hadn't been angry with him so much as the situation, but perhaps he hadn't seen it like that.

Lauren threw another glance towards the door of the Physiotherapy department then gave herself a mental shake. She knew he was conscientious about his job and she really hadn't expected her comment to stop him turning up tonight. Still, it really didn't matter whether she'd trodden on his ego or not. She had a class to teach.

'Right, ladies,' she said briskly, forcing herself to focus. 'Have any of you started to put last week's advice into practice yet?'

She laughed when everyone suddenly began speaking at once and held both hands up.

'All right! All right! One at a time!' she begged. 'How about starting at one end of the bench and working your way along?'

They all had a tale they were eager to tell and Sam, the last to speak, was no exception.

'Well, I told my boyfriend that I was doing these sessions and he dumped me,' she announced with more glee than disappointment in her voice.

'What?'

'Why, Sam?'

'Oh, what a shame,' chorused her colleagues.

'Did he say why?' Lauren asked when things grew quieter.

'He said he didn't want to go out with some butch musclewoman. He preferred his girlfriends to be feminine, and willing to trust him to take care of them.'

This time it was a chorus of groans.

'And what did you say?' Lauren asked, hiding her smile while she let the bubbly youngster entertain them.

'I told him that he wasn't around twenty-four hours a day and I was certain that if any mugger was going to attack me he wasn't going to wait until *he* was around to play the hero. I also told him I didn't think he was much of a hero if he couldn't stand the thought of a woman standing up for herself.'

'And on that note,' Lauren said over the sound of congratulatory cheers, 'it's time you *did* learn how to stand up for yourselves. If you'd like to come over onto the mats and pair up, I'll demonstrate four quick and relatively easy ways to get away if someone grabs hold of your clothing.'

By the end of their allotted hour Lauren was exhausted.

The group was so keen to learn and were picking up the techniques so quickly that she'd been able to progress from clothing releases to the techniques for making an attacker release their hold on the victim's hair. She'd also had time to run through the basics of how to deal with an attacker who tried to immobilise his victim from behind, but knew she was going to have to demonstrate again next week in slow motion.

She waved goodbye to the last of them as she collected her notes, not letting herself think that the whole session would have been so much easier if Marc had turned up again.

Not that she wanted him looking over her shoulder all the time, but she couldn't help missing the rapport she'd thought they'd started to build between them.

Or was she fooling herself? she wondered as she took a last look around the room to ensure that everything had been left as tidy as when they'd arrived.

He was such a self-contained man, his face hardly allowing the slightest hint of what he was thinking...except perhaps for the distrust that had permeated his attitude towards her from the first.

'How did it go?' said a voice right behind her, and she shrieked in shock, whirling to face her unexpected company.

'Don't *do* that!' she snapped, half-surprised that her heart hadn't leapt right out of her throat.

Marc stiffened visibly and from the way he pressed his lips together she realised that he was stifling a retort. Suddenly, she realised just how rude she must have sounded. He had every right to speak to her and if she'd been paying attention to her surroundings, rather than wool-gathering about the wretched man...

'I'm sorry,' she said hastily, 'but I didn't realise you were there, and when you spoke...'

'I came to apologise that I wasn't able to turn up in time for the class. How did it go? Did it make the demonstrations more difficult, not having the extra body there?'

'It went well,' she reported, glowing with satisfaction. 'Sometimes you get a fall-off in numbers after the first session, when they realise they aren't going to be turned into a judo black belt overnight, but this lot is still as keen as mustard.'

'So you didn't miss me?'

Lauren couldn't believe what she was hearing. It almost sounded as if Marc was bantering with her.

'Sam was disappointed that she wasn't going to get the chance to throw you around the room,' she reported hastily, hoping she'd covered up the sudden quiver in her voice.

Stupid girl, she chastised herself. Of course he wasn't coming on to you. He just wanted to know how the class went. It's part of his job.

'And were you looking forward to meting out some punishment? Do you enjoy the feeling of power when you send a man over your shoulder to bite the dust?'

Lauren's pulse had recovered from the shock of his appearance right behind her but it was starting to race again when she realised that there *was* a personal angle to his questions.

She couldn't think straight for a moment, especially when she was looking into those smoky grey eyes. She dragged her gaze away but the only thing worth looking at in the functional hospital corridor was the man in front of her.

Marc hadn't changed out of his smart grey suit tonight, but the fact that he'd loosened his tie and undone the top button definitely made him seem less formidable.

He'd settled one shoulder against the door-frame as though perfectly happy to spend a few minutes of his precious time with her.

'I like to stay fit and keep up my self-defence

skills, but that doesn't mean that I like inflicting pain on anyone,' she said finally.

'That answered one of the questions but not the other. *Do* you enjoy the feeling of power?'

It was a question she'd been asked before and she'd formulated a ready answer.

'Very few people, male or female, actually like being victims. Because we're usually smaller and less muscular than men, *most* women appreciate the fact that a knowledge of self-defence skills evens up the odds a bit.'

No one needed to know the real reason why she'd taken up martial arts. It might be one of the reasons why she'd become who she was today, but it was nobody's business but her own.

His eyes were watching her so intently that she began to grow a little uncomfortable. It was almost as though he was trying to read her secret thoughts.

Suddenly, he shouldered away from the wall, briskly straightening his jacket then delving into a pocket to retrieve a piece of paper.

'Actually, you were the reason why I was delayed,' he announced, much to her surprise. 'Do you remember this name?' He handed her the piece of paper.

'"Laurel Wainwright"?' she read in puzzlement, then the penny dropped. 'No, I don't think… Yes! That's what that man called me. You know, the one in the car park the night I—'

'The night you tipped me on my duff,' he finished wryly. 'You didn't have to remind me about that, did you?'

'Ego still smarting?' she teased, slightly amazed at her daring. She'd never bothered much with that male-female sparring before—hadn't really seen the point when she probably wasn't going to be staying long enough to take it any further.

He sent her a mock glower before getting back to the matter in hand.

'I thought I remembered that's what you'd said.'

'Have you found out who she is?' Lauren demanded eagerly. 'I've been wondering about that man since it happened—whether he was an exboyfriend or something—but he couldn't have been if he mistook me for her.'

'Well, whoever he is, I'm guessing he was the person who phoned me and made me too late to come to your class this evening.'

'What did he want? Did he say who he was?'

'No, but he told me who *you* were,' Marc countered.

'Pardon me, but I *know* who I am,' she said on a laugh. 'He must be some kind of nut.'

'He was a very insistent nut, too. He made me promise that I'd take his accusation seriously.'

'Accusation?' Lauren suddenly had a nasty queasy sensation in the pit of her stomach, totally unlike the strange flutterings that had taken up residence there when Marc had stopped to talk. 'What accusations?'

'According to my informant you're an impostor. You aren't Lauren Scott, fully qualified and experienced ward sister, at all. Your name is Laurel Wainwright and, far from being qualified to take on the responsibilities of a ward sister, you've only just finished your basic nursing training.'

CHAPTER FOUR

'AN IMPOSTOR?' Lauren gasped, absolutely horrified.

Whatever she'd been expecting, it certainly hadn't been that.

'But... You don't believe him, do you?' she demanded, conscious of a crushing sense of disappointment. 'You contacted all my referees before you even offered me the job. They must have told you—'

'Hey, Lauren, calm down,' Marc soothed, clearly startled by how upset she was. 'I didn't believe him for a moment, so you can smooth those ruffled feathers.'

'But you said—'

'I told you what *he* said,' Marc interrupted to point out calmly. 'And I didn't argue with him because there was clearly no point. He's obviously got some bee in his bonnet about this Laurel Wainwright, so it was easiest to get rid of him by promising I'd check you—or rather *her*—out.'

'And did you?' In spite of his reassurances, she couldn't help thinking back to the strange antipathy with which he'd viewed her from the first time they'd met. Had one of her referees said something untoward about her when he'd spoken to them? Was *that* why he'd been keeping such a close eye on her since she'd started work at Denison Memorial?

'Of course I didn't,' he said dismissively. 'I wouldn't waste my time when I already know everything on your CV checks out perfectly. Anyway, in the time you've been here everyone would soon have noticed if you weren't up to the job. Denison might not be a big city hospital but we do know what we're doing. We'd soon have picked up on it if you were only a fledgling trying to wing it.'

His calm certainty was like renewed balm to her soul, but that still left important questions.

'Then who on earth is he and why would he say something so stupid…something that's so easy to refute?'

'Either he genuinely believes what he's saying, in which case it's a simple case of mistaken identity, or it's being done out of spite. An ex-boyfriend with a grudge perhaps, or was there another member of staff at your old hospital who might want to cause trouble for you?'

'Well, nobody gets on perfectly with *everyone* they work with, especially in the high-pressure world of a big city accident and emergency department. But I don't think I made any real enemies—certainly not any who would want to travel up to Edenthwaite just to take petty revenge,' she said uncomfortably.

Suddenly Lauren was beginning to wonder just what nasty creatures might be crawling out of her past. And she'd thought she'd lived such an uncomplicated life since she'd started her nursing career.

'What about the ex-boyfriends? Any particularly acrimonious break-ups?'

'None,' she said succinctly, hoping he would just take her word for it without questioning her further. Of course, he didn't leave it alone.

'None?' he repeated with a lifted eyebrow. 'Just like that? You're that certain that you remained on friendly terms with every one of them?'

To her surprise, Lauren felt the slow tide of heat creeping up her throat and into her face and cursed silently.

She never blushed, and certainly not over something as unimportant as her chosen lifestyle.

'None, as in no boyfriends,' she clarified crisply. 'I've been concentrating too hard on my career to waste time on a wild social life.'

She couldn't help seeing the flash of disbelief in his eyes, swiftly followed by that all-too-familiar narrowing of his gaze that told her he was analysing what she'd said from at least three hundred and sixty directions.

Time almost seemed to stand still while she waited for his response, and she knew there would be one.

'I would have thought,' he said in a deceptively soft, musing way, without once taking his eyes off her, 'that there was a great deal of middle ground between leading a ''wild social life'' and cutting it out altogether.'

'Of course there is,' she agreed, keeping a pleasant smile on her face no matter how uncomfortable those keen grey eyes were making her feel. 'And either would be a matter of personal choice.'

The fact that she might want to make a completely different choice since she'd met him…

Enough!

Lauren hefted her file of notes for the classes to tuck them securely under one arm and checked to make sure that her keys were ready in the correct pocket. Now was the time to beat a strategic retreat, before he could start an inquisition to rival the first one he'd subjected her to at her initial interview for the job.

'If you'll excuse me,' she added politely, 'there's a pile of washing waiting for my attention if I'm going to have a clean uniform for the morning.'

All the way back to her little cottage she tried to figure out just how their conversation had veered into such personal territory.

'I would never have dreamed of asking him about his private life, no matter how much I wanted to know,' she muttered as she climbed out of her little car and locked it.

And she *did* want to know, dammit, she silently admitted, shutting the front door behind her with rather more force than necessary.

She stood in the middle of the tiny hallway and blew out an exasperated breath, suddenly realising how childish she was being. The fact that she hadn't heard anything in the way of gossip about Marc's marital status wasn't a good reason to be a bad neighbour.

The added catch was that she didn't dare ask anyone at the hospital for information about him in case they realised how strongly attracted she was by the man.

'Sorry,' she murmured towards the wall that joined her half of the isolated pair of cottages to the one next door.

One of these days she would have to make the effort to meet her closest neighbours—her only neighbours for nearly a mile in any direction if she was being accurate. She'd been living here for several weeks now, and apart from the postman hadn't seen a single soul coming or going.

She'd even begun to wonder if the cottage might

be a weekend home for someone who worked in the city, but the faint sound of music sometimes drifted through the old stone walls when she curled up in bed at night.

She listened for a moment but all was quiet. Hopefully she wouldn't be disturbing them by working her way through a couple of loads of laundry and running the cleaner over the carpet.

Not that there was a lot of carpet to clean in such a perfect doll's house of a place. To say it had two bedrooms was a bit of a joke. If she'd tried to put a bed in the smaller one she probably wouldn't be able to open the door. Still, she'd worked out that there'd had to be some compromises made when the bathroom had been installed.

She shuddered at the thought of trekking outside with a torch, especially with winter coming on. But according to the letting agent, it wasn't so long ago that the elderly lady who'd once owned her little home had still been using a privy at the bottom of the garden.

'Thank goodness for modern plumbing,' Lauren said fervently as she measured out the soap powder and prepared to set the second load going an hour later.

She stepped back and cast a last look around. 'One load already washed and in the tumble-dryer and the living-room and bedroom carpets cleaned.' She glanced down at herself and realised that she'd wanted to throw her tracksuit in with the second load so it would be clean for the next self-defence session.

'If I take this off now, it can be washing while I have my shower.' She hesitated a moment at the thought of stripping off in the kitchen then laughed at her own stupidity. 'I'm living in the middle of nowhere, for heaven's sake, and the curtains are all shut.'

It helped to hear the words out loud but she still found herself hurrying up the narrow stairs, not completely comfortable until the bathroom door was bolted between her and the rest of the world.

The modern electric shower looked a little incongruous in the quaint, low-ceilinged confines of an old cottage, but it was one of the things that had prompted her to grab the chance to rent the property. She couldn't remember when she'd last had time to lie back and relax in a bath, but she did enjoy the sensation of needles of steamy water pummelling away the stresses and strains of a busy day.

She'd just worked up a rich lather of her favourite shampoo and was about to rinse it away when she heard a sudden bang somewhere downstairs and the water stopped flowing.

'What on earth…?' she began, and opened her eyes to find herself in complete darkness. Then the shampoo trickled into her eyes and she yelped at the stinging pain.

Muttering several unladylike words under her breath, she stumbled out of the shower to find a towel, grimacing as she wrapped a second one around her soapy head.

The taps in the basin were still working, so she was able to splash her eyes with water to dilute the shampoo in them, but the shower and lights still refused to obey.

'There must be a power cut,' she guessed when her bedroom lights were equally dead, although why that should have happened when the autumn storms hadn't started yet she had no idea.

Why she peered out through the curtains, she had no idea. It wasn't as though there were any street-lights this far out into the country to tell her how widespread the problem was.

Except that there on the ground in front of the second half of the pair of cottages was a warm but-tery yellow square of light, proof that not only were her neighbours home but that they had power.

'I must have blown a fuse, then,' she surmised in dismay, not having a clue where the fuse box was situated.

It took her nearly half an hour of stumbling around in the dark with a very dim torch to locate a cobweb-festooned box under the stairs, and nearly as long again to work out how to replace the length of fuse wire in the appropriate place. And even then every-thing remained in darkness.

'Damn,' she said with a shiver, finally admitting that she was going to have to ask for help. 'What a way to have to go and introduce yourself to your neighbours.'

She contemplated the prospect of dragging clothes on over her chilled, soap-slick body and shook her head.

'A coat will do,' she decided as she rewrapped the towel around herself, tightening it so it wouldn't un-ravel itself at an inopportune moment.

With her front door key clutched tightly in her hand and wellington boots on her bare feet she care-fully made her way out of her slightly shabby front garden and into the far neater one next door, the au-tumn wind cutting her like a knife.

'I'm sorry to disturb you,' she muttered under her breath as she rang the bell, practising for when the door opened. Then a light flashed on over the door and, after the last hour spent in almost total darkness, it momentarily blinded her to the identity of the man who opened it.

'Good God, Lauren. What's happened to you?' demanded Marc Fletcher in shocked tones.

He stepped out to usher her inside with a solicitous arm at her elbow, and had already closed the door against the dark chill outside before she found her tongue.

'*You* live here?' she said through chattering teeth, barely registering the rolled-up shirtsleeves and lack of tie or the tousled dark hair. '*You're* my neighbour?'

It was obviously his turn to be surprised.

'*You* moved into the other cottage? When?'

'S-several w-weeks ago,' she stammered, thoroughly chilled now, in spite of her coat and the towel wrapped turban-wise around her soapy hair. The cosy warmth of his cottage hadn't begun to seep through to her bones yet. 'Before I s-started w-work at Denison Memorial.'

'No point in asking why we haven't seen each other in the meantime, then,' he said wryly. 'Not with both of us working at the hospital.'

Especially with the long hours *he* was reputed to keep, she thought, but kept the observation to herself.

'So, what brings you to my door? Do you need to borrow a cup of sugar?'

'I'd probably need a t-ton of the stuff to s-sweeten my disposition after the last hour,' she groaned. 'I'm almost certain I've blown a fuse, but I can't s-seem to fix it.'

'What fuse?' he asked with a glance towards her towel-wrapped head. 'Hair-dryer?'

'I wish it was that s-simple but it seems to be something major in the fuse box. Nothing's working in the whole house.' Lauren hated having to admit to failure, but at least she could console herself with the thought that she'd done her best before she'd come for help.

'Well, I can't claim to be an expert with electrical things,' Marc said as he reached past her to grab his own coat off the hook behind her, 'but I'll give it a go. Do you want to wait here in the warm while I try?'

Much as she would have loved to stay and thaw out, she shook her head.

'You're going to need another pair of hands to hold the t-torch. Oh, and have you got some batteries? Mine are nearly dead.' She flicked the switch on the torch she'd used to find her way to his door to demonstrate.

'I can do better than that. I bought myself a new torch the other day. One of those ones that looks like a miniature strip light. It's in the car.'

Silently, Lauren followed him as he strode out of the door, her own gait rather less dignified as she clomped along in her boots.

In no time at all they were both crammed into the space under her narrow stairs while she tried to direct the light onto his hands.

'This is a very old-fashioned fuse box,' he commented as he checked each circuit. 'I had the one in my cottage changed when I bought it. In fact, I had to have all the wiring updated when I put the electric shower in the bathroom. It reached the stage where I had to count the amount of electricity I was using before I climbed under the water otherwise the switch would trip... Ah!'

'Oh!' Lauren murmured, his words obviously registering with both of them at the same time.

'Did you have something else running at the same time as the shower?' he asked over his shoulder, suddenly leaning forward to examine the wiring more closely.

'The washing machine and the tumble-dryer,' she admitted. 'So I've tripped the switch, have I?'

There was an ominous silence before he turned partway to meet her gaze, his own eyes gleaming like polished pewter in the torchlight.

'You would only have tripped the switch if you had a more modern box, and it would have been a simple matter of resetting it until you could get an electrician to come out and make a proper job of it. Unfortunately, someone's obviously got fed up with the fuses blowing so often and has put a really heavy-duty one in.'

'Surely that would be a good thing, if it stops the thing cutting out like this?'

'Not when the wiring system is too old to cope with it,' he countered. 'It's a bit like... Oh, imagine a frail eighty-year-old man with a heart transplant from a twenty-year-old who then tries to enter the Tour de France.'

Lauren couldn't help giggling at the graphic illustration.

'So what you're saying is my eighty-year-old's

wiring gave out when I tried to make it work too hard.'

'Exactly,' he said as he shut the box and prepared to back out of the cramped space.

'So what do I have to do to it tonight to get it working well enough to get things working one at a time?'

'No can do,' he admitted. 'The wires have actually melted, so they're going to need replacing before they'll do what you want.'

'What!' she wailed in dismay. 'I've got two loads of washing to finish before I can go to work tomorrow and I'm still covered in shampoo. I was under the shower when the power cut out and I hadn't finished rinsing my hair.'

They were standing so close together that Lauren actually saw the impact of her words: the slight flaring of his nostrils as he breathed in the soapy scent and the way his pupils dilated at the realisation that she might be less than fully clothed under her coat.

When his eyes flicked down to the V of naked skin at the neck of her coat she almost reached up to hold the lapels together. She knew exactly where his thoughts had gone and suddenly she wasn't cold any more. In fact, she felt almost as warm as when she was standing under the pelting heat of the shower.

'You'd better come next door,' he said suddenly, and she forgot how to breathe.

'Next door?' she repeated stupidly, and cringed at the squeaky voice that emerged.

'Well, it doesn't look as if we're going to be able to get your electricity going any time soon and you need to get your laundry done.'

Thank goodness he'd turned to lead the way into

her kitchen. At least he wouldn't be able to see the blush now scalding her face.

What an idiot, to think that he'd been proposition-ing her after a single glimpse of her throat! And she was looking so alluring, too, with her soapy hair straggling out around her face from the sagging towel she'd wrapped around it.

It didn't take long to transfer the nearly dry clothes into the laundry basket and the wet ones into several carrier bags.

Lauren was following him towards her front door when he suddenly stopped.

'It would be a good idea if you grabbed some clean clothes straight away,' he suggested.

'Why?' She hefted the basket in her arms. 'These won't take long now.'

'Well, you don't want to wait around in your towel while they dry, do you? You could finish your shower at my place and get comfortable.'

The thought of climbing into Marc's shower sent a strange sensation flooding over her, a prickling, as if all the tiny hairs were standing on end at the implied intimacy.

'Uh, you don't mind?' she gulped, having to force the mental image of a totally naked Marc Fletcher sharing the shower with her out of her mind.

'Would I have suggested it if I did?' he said with a hint of exasperation. 'Hurry up if you want to get to bed before midnight.'

Lauren was having even more trouble trying to ignore pictures of Marc's naked body stretched out across a king-sized bed as she rummaged through her drawers for some clean underwear.

She groaned when she realised that, with so much

in the laundry, there was very little selection left. She discarded the ecru concoction with the dodgy catch that kept unfastening itself at the most inopportune moments, wondering why she'd bothered to keep it.

All there was left was a scandalously scanty black lace set she'd been given for her birthday by her old A and E colleagues and a silky white set with an underwired bra that created so much uplift that it made her look as if she was smuggling melons under her jumper.

Both selections still sported their original swing tags as she'd never had occasion to wear them, but when the option was choosing one of them or going braless in Marc's company...

She grabbed the black lace set and added it to the jeans and jumper she'd set out on the bed, then rolled everything up tightly to conceal the evidence.

'Don't forget your wash kit,' Marc called up the stairs. 'And lock your door on the way out. I'll go and get this lot in the machine.'

Just the thought of Marc handling her clothing was enough to have Lauren racing around. She was in such a rush to get next door in time to do the job herself that she nearly forgot to grab her keys on the way out.

'Locking myself out would *really* impress him,' she muttered as she slopped and slipped her way out of her front garden and into his.

She raised her hand to knock on the door and saw that he'd left the key in the lock for her.

'Hello?' she called as she stuck her head around the door.

'Come straight through,' he called back. 'This cottage is the mirror image of yours so you can't get lost.'

She hurried towards his voice, hoping to forestall him loading the machine, but he was just emptying the second bag of sodden clothing.

'Do you need any powder in this or had it got as far as rinsing?' he asked as he shut the door and straightened up.

'I think it just needs to finish rinsing, thanks,' she said as she came forward with the basket of half-dry clothes. 'It had been running for a while before everything died.'

'Do you want me to load those in the dryer for you?' he offered.

'I can manage, thanks,' she said hastily, swinging the basket out of his reach. Unfortunately, the sudden manoeuvre dislodged the rolled-up bundle of clothing resting on top of the basket. With a sense of dreadful inevitability she watched it plummet towards the floor where it exploded open to deposit the scandalous black lace garments at his feet.

There were several seconds of startled silence while they both gazed down at the blatantly sexy lingerie, then, with a strangled groan, Lauren dashed forward to scoop them up.

Unfortunately, Marc bent down at the same time and their heads collided with a resounding thud.

'Ouch!' Lauren clapped a hand to her head while the basket of laundry tipped out of her grasp, scattering a multicoloured assortment of damp underwear across the floor.

'Oh, good grief!' she muttered, dropping to her knees to scrabble the pile back into the basket. She nearly scooped her dry clothing in with it, only remembering at the last minute to look for the black lacy set.

'Here,' he said, reaching out towards her with the fragile scraps dangling from blatantly male fingers. 'Are you looking for these?'

'Ah, yes,' she said in a strangled voice as she tried to straighten up to take them. She stumbled briefly and it wasn't until she felt her towel drape itself around her ankles that she realised she must have been kneeling on it and had untucked its precarious folds.

She closed her eyes, unable to believe that every embarrassing nightmare she'd ever had was coming true.

'Lauren,' Marc began in a noticeably husky voice, then had to stop and clear his voice. 'I think it would be a good idea if you went up to have your shower.'

'I'll just put these on to dry,' she muttered, certain that her face couldn't have been any hotter without bursting into flames. It was almost a relief to turn her back on him while she stuffed the rest of the laundry into the tumble-dryer and examined the controls.

'It's the same make as mine,' she commented inanely as she set it going. All she wanted to do was scuttle next door without having to face him. Tomorrow morning would be quite soon enough for that, but she had two loads of washing to wait for.

She stepped back and trod on her towel, not that she needed the damp lump to remind her that she was totally naked under her coat. She'd never been so aware of her body before or the way the satin lining slid against her skin, and it was all *his* fault, standing there with his smoky grey eyes turning to pewter.

'If it's all right, I'll just borrow your bathroom for a minute,' she said when she finally managed to drag her gaze away.

In too much of a state to wait for an answer, she grabbed her dry clothes and scuttled up the stairs. She'd never felt like this before and wasn't certain that she liked it. She felt so totally out of control, *everything* felt out of control—her pulse, her breathing, her knees, even her skin didn't feel as if it belonged to her any more.

'Get a grip,' she groaned as she bolted the bathroom door and leaned back against it. 'He's going to think you're a total fruitcake if you carry on like this. So, he thinks you're in the habit of wearing sexy underwear. So what? You wouldn't be the first nurse to make herself feel better about wearing a uniform all day by hiding something slinky underneath it. And as for the towel, you'd already told him the shower cut out while you were washing your hair. He must have realised you were wrapped in a towel right from the first.'

She was still thinking about that when she climbed under the blissfully hot water and finally got rid of the stickiness of the remaining shampoo.

If Marc *had* realised she'd been wrapped in nothing more than a towel, why had he reacted that way when she'd lost it on his kitchen floor? Perhaps he just hadn't put two and two together. Perhaps that had been his first inkling that she'd been naked under her coat.

Perhaps that was why he hadn't been able to take

his eyes off her, why his voice had sounded so husky...

In spite of the heat of the water Lauren shivered, not really certain how she felt about that.

She didn't think she'd seen anything like that sort of expression on a man's face before, especially when he was looking at her. Her only other experience had been very different and a long time ago and it certainly hadn't made her feel like this.

She turned off the water and drew in a deep breath, concentrating on releasing it slowly as she found the calm centre within herself.

'That was *then*,' she whispered fiercely, needing to hear the words out loud. 'You're twenty-eight now, and you're nobody's victim. You can take care of yourself.'

She drew in another breath and when she felt her pulse begin to slow she reached for the neatly folded towel draped over the back of a bentwood chair.

'Anyway, I was probably mistaken. Marc's not interested in me that way, any more than I am in him,' she muttered as she buried her face in the towel. Then she breathed in and realised that this must have been a towel that Marc had used because she could smell the indefinable mixture of soap and musk that she would have been able to identify blindfolded.

And suddenly her pulse was racing again and she had to admit that she'd lied.

She *was* interested in him, more than she'd ever been in any other man.

CHAPTER FIVE

WHEN Lauren finally came back down the stairs it was to the sound of the washing-machine spinning.

It wasn't until the machine switched itself off that she could hear a voice coming from Marc's sitting room. It took only a moment for her to realise that he wasn't watching the television but speaking to someone on the phone.

'I'll see you at the hospital in about twenty minutes, then,' he was saying as she hurried towards the newly silent machine, fearful that he might come out to see her there and think she'd been deliberately eavesdropping.

The tumble-dryer had finished, too, and it was the work of seconds to empty it and transfer the second load from the washing machine.

'Roll on, summer,' she murmured as she began folding the warm dry pile of clothing. She far preferred the smell of things dried out in the fresh air.

'Wishing your life away?' Marc said, and nearly sent her into orbit.

'Don't *do* that!' she exclaimed. 'I hate it when people creep up on me.'

'It's a bit difficult to make a lot of noise when I'm not wearing my hobnailed boots,' he said with a meaningful glance at the footwear he was carrying.

Lauren was startled to see that he must have taken his shoes and socks off since she'd disappeared upstairs, then amazed to find herself fascinated by the vulnerability of his bare feet. Was there nothing about the man that wasn't perfectly elegant, even in a comfortably worn pair of denims?

She watched silently while he sat down to don both socks and shoes, almost forgetting to listen to what he was saying.

'I've got to go in to the hospital—there's been a problem with security,' he explained briefly. 'I'm not sure how long I'll be, but it shouldn't be more than an hour or so.'

'I didn't realise that administrators had to be on call, too. I'm sorry. Do you want me out of the way so you can lock up?' She could always keep an eye open for his return so she could come back for the second load.

'Don't be ridiculous!' he exclaimed as he shoved his arms into his jacket and grabbed his keys. 'You're perfectly welcome to make yourself at home. What on earth made you think that I'd send you back to sit in the cold and dark?'

'Well, I just thought you'd rather not leave a stranger in your home while you were out.'

'You're hardly a stranger,' he objected as he slid his mobile phone into his pocket. 'You've been a member of staff for several weeks now.'

'And most of that time you've been glaring at me as if you weren't happy about the fact,' she countered, her firm control over her tongue suddenly slipping for a fateful second.

She saw the surprise flash across his face, as if she'd overturned some preconceived idea he held in his mind, then it was gone so swiftly that she could almost persuade herself that she hadn't seen it.

'I'm very happy to have appointed such a well-qualified nurse, and equally happy with the way you've fitted in at Denison,' he said formally.

'Well, excuse me for pointing it out,' she said, deciding that she may as well get it all off her chest now that she'd started, 'but you certainly haven't given that impression. In fact, the way you've been keeping tabs on me and the suspicious looks you've been throwing in my direction, it's as if you think I'm going to poison my patients rather than take care of them.'

'That's a bit melodramatic, even for you,' he said impatiently as he glanced at his watch, apparently oblivious to the fact that her blood was slowly climbing up to a boil.

'And that's ultra-dismissive, even for you,' she countered. 'You know perfectly well that you've gone out of your way to keep an eye on me ever since I started work, and even though you've admitted that I'm good at my job, you still don't seem to trust me. Don't you think I deserve to know why?'

Her direct challenge made him turn back from the door to face her. This time the expression on his face was less easy to read, a combination of embarrassment and unease with more than a hint of resignation.

'Probably,' he said bluntly. 'But I can't stop now. I've got the night security man waiting for me.'

'When you return?' she suggested, then wondered if she was pushing her luck. Was he expecting her to go straight back to her own cottage once her laundry was dry?

'OK.' He sighed and raked a hand through the neat dark strands of his hair and the light gleamed off the sprinkling of grey just beginning at his temples. 'I suppose it *would* be better if we cleared the air.'

Suddenly Lauren felt almost guilty for putting the man on the spot. She knew he worked tremendously long hours, otherwise she'd have known before now that he lived next door to her. Perhaps his antipathy was some sort of personality clash, in which case it was proof that the fact that she found herself increasingly attracted to him was a totally one-sided thing.

Out of the blue she wondered if he'd had time for a meal since he'd come home. If not, by the time he returned from the hospital again he'd be running on fumes.

'Have you eaten yet?' she demanded as he opened the door. 'I'm sure I've got something in the freezer that we could share.'

'You'd best leave your freezer alone until you know how long it's going to be until you've got power again. I'll find something to cook when I get back.'

'If you ever leave,' she pointed out, shooing him away with a gesture. 'Go and find out what's gone wrong at the hospital.'

He groaned when he caught sight of the time. 'I'll be back as soon as I can.'

Lauren only waited until his car lights had disappeared along the lane before she started exploring his fridge for ideas. At least she didn't have to wonder whether he had any preferences or allergies. If it was in his kitchen it was something he had chosen.

And she didn't allow herself to feel the slightest bit guilty as she prepared and chopped a selection of vegetables and mixed her own version of sweet and sour sauce. With a couple of chicken breasts sliced and ready to stir-fry, it would only take a matter of minutes to have a hot meal ready when he returned.

It was closer to two hours than one and her laundry had long been finished and folded neatly into the basket by the time Lauren heard the sound of his car turning into the driveway.

With everything ready to go, she already had the kitchen full of the mouth-watering aroma of frying onions and meat when he let himself in the front door.

'You didn't have to do that,' he said as he shrugged his way out of his coat.

'Would you rather I stopped?' She paused with the wooden spatula suspended over the pan.

As if in answer to her question Marc's stomach gave a sudden loud rumble. They both laughed.

'I'll take that as a signal to continue,' she said with a lingering grin and began stirring again, quickly adding the chopped vegetables. By the time the mushrooms and stir-fry sauce had joined the rest of the ingredients Marc had opened a bottle and was pouring something into two tiny porcelain cups.

'What's that? Sake?' she asked when she turned with a plate in each hand and saw what he was doing.

'Yes. Do you like it?' He put the top on the bottle and stood it in the middle of the table beside the soy sauce she'd put there earlier. 'I was introduced to it by a Japanese colleague who presented me with several bottles.'

'I've never tried it. I know it's fermented rice wine, but is it very fierce?' She smiled distractedly as he held her chair for her, slightly uncomfortable with the unexpected attention.

'Taste it and see,' he invited as he settled himself opposite her. 'So much oriental food has such subtle flavours that I find the sake a good accompaniment. It doesn't swamp what you're eating.'

Lauren had to agree, but wasn't certain whether it was something she would want to have on a regular basis. It was, however, the basis for a discussion about their tastes in foreign cuisine and their relative skills in the kitchen.

It wasn't until some while later that Lauren realised just how long she'd been imposing on his time.

'I really ought to be going home. You've probably got your alarm set for some ghastly time in the morning.'

'I'm not so old and decrepit that one late night would kill me,' he said indignantly, then grew serious. 'Actually, that's something we need to talk about.'

'How old and decrepit you are?' she teased light-heartedly, expecting him to respond the same way after the relaxed atmosphere of the last hour or so.

Marc didn't smile back and her cheeks heated with swift embarrassment at the thought that she might have overstepped the bounds of their fledgling relationship.

Relationship? she scoffed silently, knowing she was fooling herself. They were barely acquainted, no matter what her hormones thought.

'No, it's about the reason why I was called in to the hospital this evening,' he said sombrely. 'You haven't been here very long so you probably haven't heard about it, but we had a problem with a stalker not too long ago.'

'A stalker?' Lauren blinked in surprise. She'd heard about such things happening—who could avoid it when the press had trumpeted the new laws brought in to prevent such things? The last thing she'd expected was that it might happen in such an idyllic place.

'Was that in Edenthwaite or in the hospital itself?' she asked, beginning to wonder where the conversation was going. He was actually making it sound as if it had something to do with *her*.

'In the hospital, to start with. It's a bit of an involved story but a locum doctor was stalking one of the nurses.'

'But he *was* caught?'

'Oh, yes. And he's still residing in one of Her Majesty's less regal residences, undergoing psychiatric help.'

'If he's in prison, what's that got to do with this evening?' she demanded. She had that uncomfortable prickle at the base of her skull that told her she wasn't going to like what was coming.

'Well, after he was apprehended, we set certain safeguards in place and made sure the security staff followed procedures... Oh, you don't need to know all the details. Just that this evening, one of the security staff had his suspicions aroused when he spotted someone where they shouldn't be.'

'And?' She knew he had to explain a certain amount, but all she wanted was to get to the punch line.

'It was a man coming out of the female staff cloakroom on the ground floor of north wing, but before he could get to him, the man had run off.'

'And?' she repeated. She was going to shake the man if he didn't hurry up.

'When the security man investigated, he found that

the man had managed to jimmy open a couple of the lockers, including yours.'

'Well, I don't know what he was looking for but he won't have got away with much out of mine,' she said prosaically. 'I only usually keep a spare uniform in it—and my handbag when I'm on duty. I'd already brought my laundry home to wash and obviously took my bag with me, so tonight he'd have come up totally empty-handed.'

He grimaced. 'Actually, you'd left a couple of items of junk mail on the shelf at the top, and that seems to be how he knew where to leave his note.' He got up to go over to his coat.

'Note?' Lauren's stomach dropped towards her feet. She'd thought he'd been telling her that the man had been trying to steal something from the staff lockers, not put something in. Now it seemed as if he was telling her that her locker had been targeted for some reason. 'What note? What did it say?'

She saw Marc retrieve a single folded sheet of paper from an inside pocket. He returned to the table and held it out.

She unfolded it and scanned the neatly typed words, then pored over them again, one by one, frowning as she tried to make sense of them.

'Laurel, you know this charade is childish and pointless,' she read. 'For everybody's sake it is time to do as you are told.'

'That's a photocopy of the original,' Marc pointed out, breaking into her puzzlement. 'I took the liberty of putting the original into an envelope in case there were any fingerprints on it.'

'Fingerprints?' she repeated, wide-eyed, startled

out of her examination. Why on earth would he want
to preserve fingerprints on an incomprehensible note?

It was almost as if he'd followed her thoughts.

'Because of the previous incident in the car park,
then the phone call and now the implied threat in
that note, I notified the police. They'll be coming to
the hospital to interview you at some stage tomorrow
morning. They'll probably want to take the original
note away for forensic examination, just to be on the
safe side.'

'The police?' She was turning into a parrot, re-
peating everything Marc said. Had shock robbed her
brain of independent thought?

'Think about it, Lauren,' he said persuasively.
'Whoever is doing this has used the same wrong
name each time. There's some sort of mistaken identity thing going on here, and the sooner it's sorted
out, the sooner I can stop worrying about you.'

He was worrying about her?

Just the idea was enough to make her feel all warm
inside. How long had it been since someone had
cared enough to worry about her safety? Sometimes
it seemed very hard to remember that far back.

'It certainly isn't a good advertisement for the security at Denison Memorial if members of staff can
be accosted in the car park, or their lockers broken
into,' he continued, and her happy mood disappeared
like a balloon burst by a pin.

Of course, it wasn't *her* he was worried about. It
was his precious hospital, first, last and always.

'And you work very hard to maintain Denison's
safety record,' she said quietly, earning herself a
sharp look. 'So, what time do I need to get to work
tomorrow? I'll set my alarm as soon as I get home.'

'That's the other thing we need to talk about,' he said, and this time *he* was the one who looked slightly uncomfortable. 'I don't think it would be a good idea for you to go home tonight.'

'Not go home?' She was back to being a parrot again, but it had honestly sounded as if he was suggesting she stay the night with him.

'Well, apart from the fact that it's October and you've got no heat or light in there, there's the fact that a five-year-old could probably break into your cottage if he put his mind to it.'

'What?' she gasped. 'How on earth do you know that? You were hardly in the place long enough to tell, especially as you spent most of that time with your head in the cupboard under the stairs.'

'I know considerably more about the place than that because I was hoping to buy it. I'd actually had a detailed survey done on it to know what I was up against.'

'But I thought you owned *this* place? Are you just renting, like me?' She gave a quick glance around his kitchen again. When she'd been cooking she'd noticed that it contained far more up-to-date equipment than her own. She'd automatically assumed that it must be his.

'No, I do own it, but once I'd bought the other half I was intending to knock the two together to make some of the rooms a bit more spacious. Unfortunately, by the time I got all my ducks in a row, you'd signed a rental agreement and I'd missed my chance.'

Lauren felt a twinge of guilt, then suppressed it swiftly. She hadn't known that he'd wanted to buy her place so she had nothing to feel guilty about.

Anyway, he might want bigger rooms, but what he had was perfectly adequate for a man living alone…unless he was planning for a future when he wouldn't be alone any more?

Now, why did *that* thought make her feel depressed?

'Anyway, as I was saying,' he continued, 'your place isn't really fit for human habitation tonight—there's no telling what electrical problems might have been sparked off when everything blew. Apart from that, somewhere in the Edenthwaite area there's the person who left that note.'

'Surely, you don't think there's the possibility that whoever left it might be trying to find out where I live,' she scoffed. 'It's just a simple case of mistaken identity.'

'Are you willing to risk your safety on that?' he challenged quietly. 'Wouldn't it make more sense to accept the offer of a bed until you've had a chance to speak to the police?'

Although he couldn't possibly know the reason why she was fighting the very idea of accepting his hospitality, he must have been able to see that she was still willing to argue the point.

'It's a warm bed in a warm room,' he added persuasively. 'And I'll even throw in the offer of breakfast tomorrow morning.'

It wasn't the offer of breakfast so much as the wicked smile with which he offered it that finally swung the balance. There was just something about the effect of that all-too-rare phenomenon that, in spite of bone-deep fears, she couldn't resist.

'All right, then, but just for tonight,' she agreed. 'I'll need to get my night things from next door.'

'Why bother getting cold again?' he countered.
'I've got plenty of toiletries you can use and a spare
shirt if you don't like to sleep "commando".'

'Sleep "commando"? What does that mean?' she
demanded. She'd heard that he'd been in the military
but this was the first time she'd heard him using anything that sounded like military language.

'Haven't you heard the term before?' There was a
definite note of challenge in his voice as well as the
expression in his eyes. 'It's slang and means to go
naked.'

Lauren hoped he couldn't see the sudden heat that
swept up her cheeks. Had he somehow guessed about
her attraction towards him?

For just a second she contemplated the possibility
of sleeping under Marc's roof without a stitch of
clothing to cover her body, and realised she wouldn't
dare. Even the nightwear folded in the bottom of her
laundry basket was unsuitable to wear near a man
who made her pulse race and her skin tingle with
awareness.

'I hadn't heard it before,' she forced herself to
reply, battling to keep her flustered emotions out of
her voice. 'Perhaps it's supposed to imply that a person is tough enough to be a commando if they can
do without clothes?'

'Who knows how these sayings get started?' he
said dismissively, apparently taking it for granted
that she'd agreed to stay. 'Will you need to use an
iron on the uniform you want to wear tomorrow? If
not, I can take you straight up and show you the
bedroom.'

'I will need the iron,' she said gratefully, still uncomfortable with the idea of staying any longer than

strictly necessary in Marc's home. 'You don't need to give me a guided tour. I'm sure you had things you wanted to do before I rudely interrupted your evening. Just tell me which room you want me to use and I can find my way. After all, my place is the mirror image of yours.'

He conceded with a silent nod of his head. 'In that case, you'll be in the room that faces out on the front garden. Oh, and the ironing board is on hooks on the back of that cupboard door and the iron is on the shelf just to your right inside the cupboard.'

Lauren was uncomfortably aware that he was watching her every movement as she erected the ironing board then retrieved the iron and plugged it in, but when she finally turned around the doorway was empty.

'Over-active imagination,' she muttered crossly as she grabbed the folded tunic off the top of the pile and set to work. He certainly moved silently for such a powerful-looking man, no mean feat in a creaky old cottage like this.

Her immaculate uniform was draped neatly over one arm, carefully covering the clean underwear she'd remembered she would need for the morning, when she tapped on the partly opened door to his sitting room. Good manners dictated that she should offer her thanks for his enforced hospitality and wish him good-night.

'You don't need to knock,' he said when she stuck her head around the door, the book he'd been reading now lying forgotten in his hand. 'Come in and make yourself comfortable.'

For just a moment she was tempted. His kitchen-diner was neat and functional but this room was far more welcoming in spite of the fact that it seemed to have no personal mementos on display. The big reclining chair he was sitting in certainly looked comfortable.

'Actually, I'll go on up, if you don't mind. I find that I function better if I can get a full eight hours of sleep every now and then.'

'Don't we all,' he said with a groan. 'I'll see you in the morning, then. Sleep well.'

Lauren was thoughtful as she went up the stairs. Could that actually have been disappointment she'd caught in his eyes when she'd said she was going upstairs? Could he have been looking forward to the prospect of a little undemanding conversation before they went to bed?

Before they went to bed? She stumbled as she replayed the words in her mind and they conjured up forbidden images of the two of them going to bed together rather than separately.

'Not possible,' she whispered as she shut the door, and was surprised when her words made her feel regret for the first time.

She hurriedly draped her clothing over the seat of the chair beside the bed before she sat heavily on the edge of the mattress to contemplate the startling discovery.

It had been years since she'd made her decision to concentrate on her career—more than twelve years, in fact—and this was the first time she'd ever wondered if it had been the right one.

She'd put the traumatic events of the past behind her a long time ago but she'd certainly never envisioned meeting someone like Marc Fletcher or the unexpected effect he'd have on her hormones.

Was this what all the searching had been about as she'd moved from one job to another? Was it possible that she was finally ready to take the next step forward?

Lauren sighed heavily, realising that it wouldn't matter how long she worried about the situation, she wasn't going to find an answer tonight.

She reached for the folded white garment waiting on the pillow, shook it out and held it against herself with a chuckle. She wasn't short, probably only five or so inches shorter than Marc, and had been worried about the brevity of any clothing he might leave for her to borrow. Obviously she'd forgotten that his shoulders were a great deal wider and more muscular than hers because the T-shirt he'd offered would easily cover all the essentials.

With teeth brushed and the well-washed softness of pure white cotton hanging right to the middle of her thighs, she flipped back the bedclothes, touched to see that the bed seemed to be freshly made with clean linen. She hadn't thought that a bachelor would think of such a thing.

She started to settle herself under the covers but as soon as her head hit the pillow and she drew in a deep breath she jerked upright, staring down at it in shock. The linen was certainly clean and fresh but…

'This is *his* bed!' she whispered shakily, and took another look around the room for confirmation with the unmistakable scent of Marc's body still filling her senses. She hadn't realised that she would recognise that unique mixture of clean soap and male musk quite so easily—had never even noticed it with any other man—but *this* one she could identify with her eyes shut.

Why hadn't she realised before that he'd given her his room? She certainly knew from the size of her own cottage that this was the bigger bedroom and it would be logical for Marc to use it as his own rather than as a spare room. And now that she was looking for the evidence there were several books on the little cabinet beside the bed as well as the brass-based lamp and an alarm clock.

And she had no doubt that if she were to open the wardrobe doors she would find a row of his plain cotton shirts, mostly white or pale blue, hanging next to the conservatively tailored suits he favoured.

'I won't be able to sleep in *his* bed,' she murmured aloud, her heart beating a sudden rapid tattoo that seemed almost loud enough to echo off the walls.

You wouldn't sleep at all if he were in it with you, a sly little voice whispered in her head, and in spite of her lack of experience she could picture *that* all too easily.

In spite of his height and the width of his shoulders there would be plenty of room for two, especially if they weren't worried about maintaining any distance between the two of them.

'Oh, stop it!' she hissed. 'That's just your hormones getting out of hand!'

As if the senior administrator of Denison Memorial would be interested in sharing the bed with her.

'He's just being a gentleman, offering me the more comfortable room,' she muttered as she settled herself under the covers again. 'Anyway, what's your alternative to sleeping in his bed? Do you want to go down to tell him you'd rather take his spare room? In his T-shirt? Is it worth getting dressed again to go down, only to find that he can be just as stubborn as you are?'

Logically, she knew that the only option was to stay where she was and be grateful for his consideration. That didn't mean that it was going to be easy to ignore the fact that last night he had been lying where her body lay now; his head had rested on the same pillow and looked up at the same ceiling.

She switched off the light and closed her eyes, but that didn't stop her brain from working.

Even as she was drifting off to sleep it was still filled with images of his powerful frame stretched out under these same covers, his legs longer than hers, long enough to reach almost to the foot of the bed, and his hands…

But then it wasn't *his* hands any more.

These hands were gripping and pinning hers together over her head…then one over her mouth to stop her screaming for help…blind panic…can't breathe…can't move…can't stop him…*must* stop him…kick him…bite him…fight him and fight some more…desperate for breath…lungs burning but can't give in…*won't* let him win…

She wrenched violently to one side and rolled over then felt herself falling. She hit the floor with a thud and lay there gasping for breath and shaking all over.

CHAPTER SIX

IT TOOK Lauren several minutes of staring wildly around in the darkness before she realised that she wasn't sixteen years old any more. Her recent ordeal had just been a terrible pointless nightmare.

'Why *now*?' she groaned, sitting up and dropping her head onto her bent knees. She tried to rake her fingers through her hair and grimaced as she felt the short strands plastered to her skull with sweat. Her makeshift nightshirt was similarly soaked and she shivered convulsively.

What on earth had made her dream about *that*, after all this time? It had been years since she'd put that episode firmly in her past, helped enormously by her own determination and the unexpected skill she'd discovered in martial arts.

Had the old fears been resurrected because she'd gone to sleep imagining Marc lying in the same bed or had it simply been the fact that she was experiencing sexual attraction for the first time? Was this going to happen every time she fell asleep thinking about him?

Experimentally, she tried to make herself remember the details of the dream but the harder she tried, the further they receded.

Puzzled, she wondered what was happening. Before, she'd had to deliberately block the images from her mind. This time, it was far easier to remember the frisson of excitement she'd felt when she'd imagined Marc beside her in the bed.

A slow smile crept over her face when she realised the implications. It seemed as if Marc—or at least her newly admitted feelings towards him—might have finally broken the last hold her old memories had over her.

The numbers on the alarm clock glowed softly in the darkness and she groaned again. It was only two o'clock in the morning. If she'd been in her own home with her power still working she'd have been able to freshen up with a shower and a change of nightwear.

As it was, she had a choice of risking waking her generous host by using his shower in the middle of the night, or making do with the lesser impertinence of searching his cupboards for a dry T-shirt.

Rummaging through his cupboards seemed the kinder option so with the bedside light on she dragged herself to her feet and shuffled her way across the partially lit room.

She was just inches away from the bedroom door when there was a definite knocking sound.

She stifled a squeak of surprise and froze at the unexpected noise. Was it ghosts? It couldn't be Marc. In spite of the fact she'd fallen out of bed, she didn't think she'd made enough noise to wake him, so he would still be fast asleep.

'Lauren? Are you all right?' his deep voice demanded softly, proof positive that she was wrong, and she swallowed a groan. How embarrassing could things get? Not only had she had a nightmare and fallen out of bed but she'd woken her host.

Still, he was speaking softly so perhaps that meant

he wasn't certain she was awake. If she kept very quiet he might think he'd been mistaken…

No. That would be rude. He'd come to see if she was all right. The least she could do was reassure him she was fine—horribly embarrassed, but fine—and make her apologies.

She opened the door just far enough for him to see her face.

'Marc, I'm so sorry I woke you up,' she began, but when she caught sight of him standing outside the door she almost swallowed her tongue.

'No need to apologise. I wasn't asleep,' he said in an almost rusty voice, and that wasn't the only thing that had changed since she'd seen him last.

She blinked as she took in the figure dimly lit by the light seeping out over her shoulder and through the gap in the doorway. Marc's neatly barbered hair looked as if he must have spent a fair amount of the intervening time ploughing his fingers through it and his clothes almost looked as if he'd been sleeping in them. Worst of all was the fact that he'd undone several buttons at the neck of his shirt and the shadowy hair across his chest looked even darker against the stark white of the fabric.

She shivered and wasn't entirely certain whether it was because she was getting chilled or because, just for a fleeting second, she'd wondered whether those dark whorls would feel silky or wiry against her fingertips.

'Lauren! What happened? Are you feeling all right?' he demanded, stepping towards her as though to get a closer look at her in the dim light.

Lauren suddenly realised that while she'd been stupidly gazing at him she must have allowed the bedroom door to swing open wider than she'd intended. Unfortunately Marc was far too observant not to notice that she looked wringing wet, his eyes swiftly cataloguing every inch from her lank damp hair to the clammy T-shirt.

'I'm all right, Marc,' she said hurriedly, stepping out of sight behind the door again.

'You don't look it,' he argued, clearly concerned if the sharp pleat between his eyebrows was to be believed. 'You look almost as if you're running a temperature.'

He reached out a hand as though to feel her forehead but she ducked out of the way.

'Well, I'm not,' she said crossly, realising that he wasn't going to drop it unless she convinced him. 'If you *must* know, I had a dream and woke up tangled in the covers. I just need to change my nightwear.'

'You look as if you need another shower first,' he countered. 'You'll catch a chill if you go back to bed like that.'

Lauren couldn't deny she'd like to freshen up, but she was guiltily aware that this was the middle of the night. They both needed their sleep.

While she tried to find polite words to refuse his suggestion, he once more acted as though the matter was settled.

'Help yourself to another T-shirt and get yourself under the shower,' he said briskly, turning towards the top of the stairs. 'I'll have a warm drink ready for you by the time you've finished.'

'Marc…' she began, but quickly realised that she might as well save her breath. He was already halfway down the stairs.

'He must have been a sergeant-major at least,' she

muttered under her breath as she grabbed the first T-shirt she came to and hurried into the bathroom. 'He's far too accustomed to handing out orders.'

Still, she admitted with a groan of pleasure, he'd been right about the shower. It really felt good to wash the sweat out of her hair and know she was getting rid of the sour smell of long-ago fear from her body.

She hadn't realised just how brief the T-shirt she'd chosen was until she opened the bathroom door and the steamy heat was dissipated by the cooler air of the hallway. Suddenly it felt as though she was completely naked up to the waist. It didn't help that she'd forgotten to take fresh underwear with her and couldn't bear to don the damp pair again now that she was clean and dry.

'Going commando, my foot!' she muttered as she reached for the towelling robe hanging on the back of the door, unwilling to chance even the short trip to her room so precariously dressed. 'That sort of macho trend sounds like too much ego and not enough common sense to me.'

Marc tried to concentrate solely on pouring hot chocolate into two mugs but it wasn't enough. All he could see in his mind's eye was the picture of Lauren Scott standing in his bedroom doorway with the light from his bedside lamp behind her.

For one breath-stealing moment he'd actually thought she'd been naked. His heart had nearly stalled with the shock then had catapulted into double-time.

She might as well have been naked for all the concealment she'd derived from that clingy short T-shirt.

He groaned as his body reacted all too predictably and tried to drag his thoughts away again but it was no good. He hadn't seen a naked woman in far too long and certainly not one who looked as good as Lauren.

Those legs were amazing. Obviously well toned from the exercise she took, they were model slender and looked long enough to go all the way up to her waist.

For a brief second he found himself imagining what they would feel like if they were wrapped around *his* waist, but that was the point at which everything ground to a halt.

'Been there, done that,' he muttered grimly, reminding himself exactly why it wouldn't be happening again. He'd had it all, once—the beautiful wife, the cherubic daughter, the perfect life. His guilt wouldn't allow him to take that sort of chance. Anyway, why would he want to run the risk of having his heart ripped out all over again?

There was no point even dreaming about starting something with Lauren. He didn't need to look at her CV again to remind himself that she was someone who didn't believe in permanence. Perhaps he should concentrate on trying to predict exactly how many weeks or months it would be before she was on the move again, off to pastures new.

Whenever it was, it would be too soon, especially if he was left to try to find someone good enough to replace her. That was almost the most frustrating part about the situation.

Knowing her track record, he'd deliberately kept an eye on her at first, quickly realising that she was an excellent nurse, well liked by staff and patients alike, and he didn't think her department had ever been better run. Then he'd realised that it wasn't Lauren the nurse he'd wanted to see when he'd headed towards her department and had deliberately curtailed his visits.

Consciously, he knew that there was no point to them, but if his recent dreams were anything to go by, his subconscious had already gone far beyond casual friendship and into the realms of passion and a longing for permanence.

Marc shook his head, firmly reminding himself that permanence wasn't a word found in Lauren's dictionary. 'Even if I were in the market for a relationship,' he added aloud as he heard the water stop running in the shower, 'friendly neighbours and work colleagues, that's all we can ever be.'

All he had to do now was remember it, he told himself sternly as he grabbed both mugs in one hand and turned the light off.

He reached the top of the stairs just as Lauren walked out of the bathroom wrapped in his towelling robe and all his resolve disappeared like the steam drifting off the top of their drinks.

All he could think about was untying the belt she'd wrapped so securely around her slender waist and finding out which of his T-shirts she was wearing. Then he wanted to strip it off her while he discovered if every inch of that body was as beautiful as he'd imagined just a short while ago.

What was it about her? What was it that Lauren had that no other woman possessed? What magic element was it that could overpower his will so effortlessly?

Even now, with her wet hair combed sleekly

against her head and not a speck of make-up to en-
hance a single feature, she was one of the most in-
trinsically beautiful women he'd ever encountered.
Not beautiful in a stereotypically picture-perfect sort
of way but in a way that affected him somewhere
inside.

It was almost as if he'd spent the last few years
waiting in suspended animation, every emotion
locked away in a frozen wasteland. Then he'd met
Lauren and there had been a seismic shift in how he
felt, a recognition that something elemental had
changed for ever.

The trouble was, he didn't know what had changed
and in what way, neither did he know whether she
had felt anything similar.

And still he had to come back to the realisation
that, no matter what he felt about her or for her,
Lauren wasn't someone who would be content to settle somewhere like Edenthwaite. He only had to remember the glowing reference her A and E consultant had given her when she'd left the big city
hospital to know that she could return to a similar
top-notch position any time she wanted.

'I hope you don't mind,' she said softly, colour
tinting her cheeks, and he wondered just how long
he'd been standing there staring at her while his
thoughts had circled round and around the same
theme.

'Mind?' He pushed the bedroom door open with
his free hand and gestured for her to go in first, wondering if he was making a monumental mistake as
he followed her into the familiar room.

He put her mug beside the lamp then stepped back
to take a sip from his own. He could tell himself that

he hadn't handed her the mug so she didn't burn herself trying to take it from him, but if he was honest, it was because he didn't dare get any closer at the moment.

'That I borrowed this.' She flipped the end of the belt securing the towelling robe and his heart gave a hopeful extra beat. 'I didn't have anything with me and your T-shirts aren't quite long enough for modesty.'

'Oh, I don't know,' he heard himself say. 'They cover just enough to give a man's imagination something to work with.'

'Marc!' she exclaimed, clearly startled, and he cursed his uncharacteristic loss of restraint. Time for some damage control.

'Well, you can always tuck yourself under the covers if you want to hide your legs. You'll be able to reach your chocolate from there, too.'

Lauren hesitated a moment then followed his suggestion, but instead of removing his robe once she was settled against the headboard she opted to keep it on, much to his adolescent disappointment.

'You know, even your uniform can't hide the fact you've got lovely legs, and a T-shirt covers far more than a swimming costume. Anyway, I'm a man,' he continued softly, finding himself deliberately seeking and holding her gaze. 'You can't expect me to be unaffected by such a beautiful woman.'

The soft post-shower bloom darkened her cheeks by several shades but even when he saw the trace of uncertainty in her eyes, she didn't look away from him.

In fact, she seemed to be just as interested in watching him and as her eyes went from his eyes to his mouth and back again, their honey colour deepened to intoxicating brandy even as he watched. Then he saw the brief flicker of her tongue against her lips and he nearly groaned aloud.

Was she trying to kill him? She certainly couldn't be as innocent as she seemed if she could heat his blood to combustion point with nothing more than a look.

Almost before he'd realised he was going to do it he'd taken the long stride forward that put him in reach of the hands wrapped around the mug of chocolate and was reaching for it.

Clumsily, he took it from her and deposited both mugs beside the lamp before sinking to the edge of the mattress.

'Lauren,' he breathed, hardly daring to touch her now that he was close enough. He knew it was wrong, but knew he would die if he didn't.

Her eyes widened as he leant towards her then drifted closed in silent surrender as his lips finally touched hers.

That was all it took.

In the space of a heartbeat she'd opened to him, her arms stealing around him hesitantly at first and then tightening as though she never wanted to let him go.

She was everything he could ever want, heat and light and joy all wrapped in one searing package.

Had he been waiting for ever for this kiss? It had certainly been years since the last time he'd kissed Erica and—

Erica!

He froze, the heat of passion doused by the icy deluge of remembered guilt. What was he doing?

'I'm sorry,' he muttered, turning his head away and loosening his hold on her.

'I'm not,' she said softly, her arms still wreathed around his neck.

'What?' He nearly groaned when he looked down into wide soft-focused eyes.

'I'm not sorry,' she said, her husky voice far from steady.

'Why?'

'Because you're a good kisser,' she said with an unexpectedly mischievous smile and tightened her arms just a little.

Marc felt the heat of a blush sweep up his throat and into his face and had to swallow a curse. Blushing at thirty-nine? What on earth would Lauren think of him?

'It's been a long time since the last time, and it's never been like that,' he heard himself admit, his brain so scrambled that even as he'd been persuading her to release him he'd been powerless to stop the words emerging.

'Really?' she breathed, so patently delighted that he was hard-pressed not to kiss her again. Unfortunately he realised only too well that he wouldn't want to stop at a kiss, and anything more just wasn't possible.

'It's late,' he said inanely as he forced himself to step away from the bed. 'We both need to get some sleep.'

'Marc?' she called softly as he stepped out of the room, but he couldn't afford to listen; couldn't trust himself to spend another minute in her company.

'Well, damn,' he swore angrily when he finally reached the seclusion of the sitting room. After all his reminders about why it couldn't happen…*mustn't* happen…

He returned to the dubious comfort of the reclining chair where he'd been sitting all evening knowing that sleep would be all but impossible while she was lying in his bed.

The isolated cottage was so quiet that the thump on the ceiling above his head had sent him hurrying up the stairs, imagining that someone had broken into the house and was attacking her while she slept—the same person who had accosted her in the car park, perhaps?

In spite of the radical change of direction he'd taken with his life, he would never be able to ignore someone who needed help and protection, and in that moment he'd been certain that Lauren needed both.

He groaned as he settled himself in the chair again and tipped it back as far as it would go, resigned to a sleepless night. Not for anything would he let Lauren know that, because he'd given up his bed to her, he would be spending the night here, in the only other 'bed' in the cottage.

'Another week gone already,' Lauren murmured as she hurried towards the physiotherapy department. At least today she'd been able to get away from the ward on time and would have a few minutes to catch her breath before her self-defence students arrived.

She pushed the door open with one shoulder, her arms full of folders for the class and bags of uniforms being taken home for washing. There were two sets today after that disastrous half-hour on the ward this afternoon. Plastic aprons were all very well but they didn't cater for the post-operational patient who overshot the kidney bowl held under her chin by a distracted junior nurse and caught you full in the back.

Poor Mrs Hallam. She'd only come in for a relatively minor procedure but she'd probably never recover from the embarrassment of being sick over the ward sister.

She shuddered at the memory and hastily put it out of her mind. At least it proved what a good idea it was to have a spare uniform waiting in her locker.

Not that she liked going to her locker these days. It might have been a week since it had been forced open, and she'd actually transferred her things to the only other unallocated one, but still she couldn't help wondering at the point of the whole thing.

Surely, by now, the man should have realised that he'd made a monumental mistake; that she wasn't this Laurel Wainwright he was looking for.

'Hello, Lauren. I was hoping to catch you before your ladies arrived,' said a voice behind her, and she promptly dropped everything she was carrying with a shriek.

'Marc!' she exclaimed in exasperation as she bent to gather everything up again. 'I'm going to have to tie a bell round your neck if you keep creeping up on me like that.'

Not that she wasn't pleased to see him. Her rapid pulse rate had far more to do with his proximity than her surprise, especially as she'd hardly set eyes on him in a week.

When his alarm had woken her the previous Tuesday morning she'd ventured downstairs to find he'd already breakfasted and left for the hospital. A brief note had invited her to help herself and lock up when she left.

Another message had awaited her when she'd arrived on the ward, giving her the name of a reliable electrician to sort out her faulty wiring, but since then, nothing.

After his absence last week she'd been certain that he wouldn't attend the class this evening either. Did his presence mean that he still didn't fully trust her after all?

'I wasn't certain whether you were going to need an extra body for demonstrations tonight,' he said, but when she should have been answering she was too busy noting the fact that he'd changed out of his impeccable business suit into casual wear.

And they weren't just any nondescript jeans and T-shirt either. The jeans were unexpectedly disreputable, obviously well washed and worn almost white in uncomfortably strategic places.

The T-shirt was plain white, unremarkable and probably identical to a million others. It contrasted strongly with his dark hair and the healthy colour of his skin and revealed more than it concealed of his unexpectedly muscular body. But as he stood there waiting for her reply she had the strange feeling that the one he was wearing was the same one he'd lent her to sleep in.

Enough! she ordered her wandering attention. 'If you've got time, that would be very useful,' she admitted, slightly uneasy with the prospect and hoping he couldn't tell. 'The whole group has been doing very well. Several of them have even met up between classes to practise what they've learned. They're probably ready for some simple throws.'

The door behind them swung open to admit the first class members, obviously keen and eager to begin.

'Hmm. Is it too late to take back my offer?' he asked with mock trepidation on his face. 'You won't set them all on me at once?'

Lauren grinned at the mental image, but then she felt a sharp stab of something strange. All she had to do was picture bright, beautiful Sam learning to flip Marc over her shoulder and she could almost feel her protective claws coming out.

Could it possibly be jealousy she was feeling? And if it was, if she didn't want even *that* much contact between him and another woman, what did that say about her feelings toward Marc?

She didn't have time to think about it now, not with the rest of the group arriving, full of banter and raring to go.

To consolidate what they'd learned the previous week and correct any errors that might have crept into their techniques, she quickly ran through the methods of release if an assailant were to grab them by their hair or clothing.

'Don't forget to keep your fist tightly clenched, Marion,' she warned as she watched the older woman practise aiming a punch. 'If you don't, your blow won't be effective and, what's worse, you'll hurt yourself.'

'You might find it easier to use the bony base of your hand,' Marc suggested as he came over to join their small group. 'Especially smaller women who are trying to aim upward at a taller opponent. Here…' He beckoned Lauren towards him. 'Aim for my nose and show her what I mean.'

Lauren felt strangely awkward as she positioned herself in front of him, far too aware of those intent grey eyes.

Although she was expecting it, she still felt a jolt of awareness when he grabbed a shoulder in each hand. She had to clear her throat before she could speak.

'As you can see, when you're this close you need to take him by surprise with a fist to the gut—tightly clenched, of course. If you think he's too fat or too well muscled for that to have much impact, aim up at his nose with the heel of your hand as if you're trying to drive his nose straight up between his eyes.'

She pulled the punch, stopping just short of contact with his nose, and had the brief satisfaction of seeing him flinch.

'If she'd landed that one,' Marc said, his breath puffing out across the bare skin of her wrist and sending shivers right up her arm, 'by now I'd have let go of her to clamp both hands over my face, and my eyes would be watering so badly that I wouldn't be able to see which way she'd run.'

'And it's such a simple thing to learn,' Marion marvelled. 'Why aren't *all* women taught self-defence as soon as they're old enough?'

'There would certainly be a lot fewer victims if they were,' Lauren agreed, then smiled to lighten the mood. 'Well, I'm doing my best, but I can only manage small classes at a time.'

'As long as you keep going with a new group every few weeks, you could have the whole of Edenthwaite trained in a few years,' Sam quipped. 'Just imagine being able to go out of an evening knowing that the local men know there's no point trying it on. We might feel as safe to go for a walk as my grandmother did years ago, before mugging became as popular as an Olympic sport.'

'The trouble is, the fact that women knew how to defend themselves wouldn't necessarily change society back to the way it was then,' Marc pointed out grimly. 'Two generations ago, it was a rare occurrence for women, babies or the elderly to be victims, and those who attacked them were totally ostracised by the rest of the population and punished for their crimes. Thugs nowadays seem to deliberately pick on those groups because they're the easier targets and people barely seem to notice any more.'

There were mutters of agreement and Lauren realised she was going to have to step in if the class wasn't going to turn into a discussion group debating the many ills of modern society.

'Right, now, ladies,' she announced, pitching her voice over the hubbub, 'the next demonstration is how to get your assailant to let go if he's grabbed your hair from behind.' She gestured to Marc, signalling that she was ready.

She was expecting him to grab a handful of her hair but she wasn't expecting to find the sensation of his fingers sliding against her scalp so pleasant. It was almost a shame to make him release her.

'Now, remember what we did when he grabbed from the front?' she prompted.

'Grab his wrist in both hands?' Sam suggested, and Lauren reached up and back to comply.

'Pull his hand tight against your head?' Marion called, and as nodding wasn't possible, Lauren smiled her agreement.

'Now comes the interesting bit,' she said. 'In slow

motion I'm going to bend forward and turn in under his arm and you watch what happens.' She suited her actions to her words and with her hands gripped around his wrist Marc had to lean forward as she did. When she turned she took him completely off balance so that he tumbled forward into a gentle somersault, automatically releasing her hair.

'Hey, that's neat!' Sam exclaimed.

'This should be the only time you get to appreciate how neat it is,' Lauren warned. 'Remember, when you're actually in that situation, as soon as you get free, run away.'

'Can you show us again?' Marion asked with a worried frown. 'Which way did you turn when you bent forward?'

Lauren positioned herself and went through the whole manoeuvre again in slow motion, this time stopping short of depositing Marc on his back.

'Spoilsport!' Sam grumbled, then sent Marc a wicked grin. 'I rather like seeing big strong men brought down to size.'

She's flirting with him! Lauren realised with a shock, and this time the pang of jealousy was unmistakable. It didn't matter that Marc must be nearly old enough to be the young woman's father, or that he hadn't responded in any way. All she could think about was that Sam had noticed what an attractive man he was under that serious professional appearance.

There were equal numbers of giggles and groans as everyone took their turn but eventually they all had the mechanics of it straight in their heads.

Lauren finished off the session with a couple of wrist locks and arm locks which she'd found particularly useful during her time in A and E. It was amazing how persuasive the threat of imminent pain could be when a drunk got stroppy and started throwing his weight around.

With one hand gripping Marc's bent elbow, she used the other to grip his wrist and twist it backwards. It wouldn't take much more pressure to force him onto his back, especially if he really had attacked her and she wasn't concerned about hurting him. All she would need was speed and the element of surprise.

'This is usually enough to keep an assailant under control until Security can come and take him out of your hands,' she announced with a straight face, but they all groaned at the deliberate pun.

The final demonstration, with a straight arm lock, would also be useful in a similar situation and was mastered in record time.

'Last class next week,' Lauren reminded them as they gathered up their belongings. 'And we'll do a complete revision of everything you've learned during the course.'

In his quiet gentlemanly way she watched Marc hold the door open for her departing class, sharing a quiet word with several.

Lauren turned away to gather up her own things, determined to get her unwanted jealousy under control if only by turning her back on the sight of all those women smiling at him.

What right did she have to feel jealous, anyway? In spite of the kiss they'd shared, the fact that he'd made no attempt to speak to her in the week since it had happened was enough to reinforce the point that there wasn't any sort of relationship between the two of them. He obviously felt perfectly free to smile at anyone he pleased.

She busied herself putting her spare sets of notes away in their folder, her thoughts chasing each other around in her head no matter what she did to switch them off.

The first she knew that she wasn't alone in the room was when someone put their hand on her shoulder.

CHAPTER SEVEN

AFTER an hour and a half of concentrating on teaching and practising defensive manoeuvres, Lauren didn't even have to think.

Automatically, she reached up and wrapped both hands around her assailant's wrist and with a speed and force that she'd never have dreamed of using on a volunteer, bent forward and twisted to send the man sailing over her shoulder.

Even as he crashed in an ignominious heap at her feet she was whirling to run for the door, but then her brain kicked in to override her reflexes.

Suddenly she realised who it was she'd just summarily flipped onto his back.

'Marc!' she exclaimed in horror, immediately rushing forward to see if he was all right.

Had she injured him? She'd certainly thrown him hard enough to give him a whole host of bruises. And he was making no attempt to get up by himself, hadn't even moved, and that worried her. Had he landed hard enough to break something? Fractured a vertebra, perhaps? Had she paralysed him?

To her relief, when he finally took her hand his grip seemed as firm as ever and she allowed herself a brief surge of relief, but she was still concerned enough that she wondered if she should suggest that he go for an X-ray.

Before she could brace herself to help him to his feet he suddenly gave a swift tug, catching her totally unprepared. With one brief shriek she tumbled help-lessly forward, landing straight on top of him with enough force to empty her lungs.

Frozen with disbelief, she found herself sprawled across his chest with her nose buried in the angle between his neck and shoulder.

It took several endless seconds before she even thought about trying to draw a breath, then wished she hadn't bothered. The scent of his skin was every bit as enticing as she remembered and as for the lean, muscular body trapped underneath her...

'Oh!' she gasped, struggling to peel herself off him, suddenly all too aware of the way their legs were entwined.

'Whoa!' he said, swiftly grasping her waist in both hands so that she couldn't move.

'What are you *doing*?' she demanded breathlessly, lifting her head far enough to glare down at his face. 'Why did you do that?'

'Just evening the score out a bit,' he said with an unexpectedly wicked glint in his quicksilver eyes. 'You've been throwing me around all evening so turnabout's fair play.'

'Very funny,' she snapped, renewing her struggle. 'Now let me up.'

'Hang on, Lauren.' He swiftly tightened his grip again to hold her still. 'Let's do this carefully, please. I have no wish to sing soprano.'

All of a sudden she realised exactly which area her knee was threatening and she cringed with em-barrassment, her face almost incandescent with heat.

Even though she wished fervently that she could disappear into thin air, she had no idea what he wanted her to do so she had to remain perfectly still.

Her nose was almost buried in the V neck of his T-shirt now, and one crazy corner of her brain was noting that she had a close-up view of the start of those tantalising dark whorls of hair. For one mad second she even contemplated rubbing her cheek against them to find out once and for all just what they felt like, but didn't dare move.

When Marc didn't move either, she had to know what was happening and lifted her head again.

His eyes were waiting to meet hers, the silvery grey darkening even as she watched.

'Lauren?' he murmured, but if it was a question, she had no idea of the answer.

Suddenly he tightened his grip again, wrapping his arms completely around her, and then he was rolling the two of them over so that she was the one who ended up on her back and he was spread-eagled over her.

He stared down at her for a moment that stretched into infinity and she could see the battle he was fighting with himself. She held her breath, trying to tell herself that she didn't care one way or another, then she saw his head angle towards her and she knew she'd lied.

Then his lips met hers in the briefest and most gentle of kisses, just a fleeting impression of sweetness and warmth. It was perfect and yet almost as soon as it started it was over and she was definitely disappointed when he lifted his head again. She'd wanted so much more.

He must have read that disappointment in her eyes because he only hesitated for a split second longer before he lowered his head again.

Just before his lips met hers she saw his eyes close,

the dark fans of his lashes looking almost vulnerable against the lean planes of his face, and she was help-less to do anything different. Every nerve in her body seemed to be concentrating on the flood of sensations pouring through her as he brushed his mouth over her trembling lips then nipped at them as though hun-gry for more.

Mesmerised, she parted them, not really under-standing what she was doing or what signal it might be giving. Then she felt the merest flicker of his tongue over her lower lip, a tasting, almost an ex-ploratory foray before the full searing possession that followed.

She would never have believed that something as simple as a kiss could go from gentle warmth to nu-clear meltdown in a single second, and she was to-tally overwhelmed. This was so far outside anything she'd ever experienced before that she whimpered, helpless to know how to respond.

'Marc,' she gasped when his lips burned a path down her throat, not stopping till he reached the breast he held cupped in the palm of his hand.

Even through the layers of clothing the heat of his breath seared her and when he took her into his mouth the sensation was so exquisite that she couldn't help moaning aloud.

As if the sound had been a signal, Marc instantly released her and rolled away with a muttered impre-cation.

Shock at his sudden desertion held her immobile for several seconds but then Lauren instinctively curled into a defensive ball, desperately trying to control her trembling awareness of the man who had just shown her a glimpse of heaven only to snatch it away.

She felt a single betraying tear trickle from the corner of her eye and run across her temple to soak into her hair.

Inside she was cringing, certain she'd made an utter fool of herself. Why didn't he go? She certainly didn't want to face him tonight. What could she say?

'I'm sorry, Lauren,' he murmured softly, but there was a definite edge to his voice. 'Really…that should never have happened. I had no right…'

She didn't know what to say.

For a dozen years she'd almost completely denied her womanhood, telling herself that her career was more important. Then she'd met Marc Fletcher and over the last few weeks her awakening had begun.

Then, tonight, in such a prosaic place as a hospital physiotherapy department he'd revealed the secret magic to her. For just a moment he'd given her wings and shown her how to fly…only to bring her back to earth with a shattering crash.

If he hadn't wanted to fly with her it would have been kinder if he'd left her in ignorance. Now she'd always know what she was missing—yet another in the long list of things that would be for ever missing in her life.

Silently, the single tear was joined by another and then a flood and she really didn't care whether Marc was there or not.

It wasn't just *this* disappointment she was crying for but all the disappointments large and small that had buffeted her throughout her twenty-eight years, from the death of her parents to the abusive foster-brother to the loneliness of the solitary life she'd forced herself to live.

'Oh, Lauren, don't,' he said. She tensed when she realised he was still nearby, but then he pressed a handkerchief into her hand.

'Thanks,' she managed to whisper, strangely grateful that he hadn't deserted her to her misery, but anything more was beyond her. It seemed that once the floodgates opened, nothing could stop the flow until the reservoir was dry.

It took longer than she would have imagined but finally she searched out a dry corner on the sodden fabric to blow her nose, knowing it was for the last time.

'I'm sorry,' she croaked, her voice all but gone. Probably rusted away by all the salt, she thought as she forced her swollen eyes open far enough to peer at Marc to find he'd positioned himself protectively between her sobbing form and the doorway to the department.

She closed her eyes for a moment to savour the unfamiliar flood of warmth that realisation brought. How many years had it been since someone had wanted to shelter her, protect her? Not since her parents had been taken from her in that freak accident on black ice, probably. She certainly couldn't remember an incident since then.

Except since she'd met Marc...

If she counted the night he'd insisted she sleep in his bed, this was the second time he'd inconvenienced himself just for her.

Why?

It certainly wasn't in keeping with the suspicious way he'd regarded her right from the first time he'd met her. His attitude then had been almost as though he'd suspected her of having designs on the family silver. Had his regard for her changed so much that he was willing to sit still and quiet while she cried her heart out?

She didn't know what had changed or how or why, but she did know she was grateful. Just knowing he was there, somewhere nearby…she'd never be able to put into words how much that meant to her.

'Thank you,' she croaked, forcing her eyes open to meet his in the hope that he would see how much she meant the simple words.

'No thanks required,' he said with a single shake of his head. 'You obviously needed that and I'm sorry if it was my fault that it happened like that…that I triggered it off. The least I could do was be there for you.'

There was such depth of meaning in his voice that she knew he'd suffered emotional trauma, too. She wondered if there had been someone there for him when he'd cried out his grief.

Or had he cried it out?

Lauren had no idea what had put that thought into her head but the more she examined it the more she wondered if that was what surrounded his emotions like an unseen grey cloud. Were the shadows in those smoky grey eyes an old pain that had never been resolved?

'Can I help you up?' he asked, snapping her out of her fanciful thoughts.

She looked up at him to see him crouching beside her, his hand opened towards her.

Hesitantly, she placed her hand in his, marvelling

at the difference in size and power as hers all but disappeared in his grasp.

She straightened up and then wobbled ignominiously, as though the tears had robbed her of all her strength.

'Legs like overcooked spaghetti,' she muttered, grateful for the second hand that grasped her elbow to steady her.

'Will you be all right?' he asked solicitously. 'If you're too wobbly I could carry you out to my car, if you like.'

Lauren had a brief mental image of being swept off her feet like some Gothic heroine then had to chuckle. 'Wouldn't *that* go down well on the hospital grapevine. We'd never hear the end of it. Anyway, I can't leave my car here. I'll need it in the morning.'

'If you're sure.' He smiled, too, but she suddenly realised that he'd meant the offer seriously. And she doubted that the thought of what anyone would say about it would have made him take it back.

'Honestly, I don't need to be carried. I was just a bit unsteady for a minute,' she reassured him, almost disappointed at the missed opportunity.

Then she had another mental image, one that *was* possible and that she was only now realising that she needed far more.

'Marc...' she began hesitantly. 'I know it's late and...and you've been very patient while I...fell apart all over the place...but...'

'I don't deserve your gratitude, Lauren,' he said firmly. 'If I hadn't overstepped the bounds like that, you'd already be home by now. Anyway, I had nothing better to do this evening than allow myself to be flung around—unless you wanted to condemn me to more hours of poring over financial statements and wage forecasts. If there's something you want, just spit it out and I'll do my best.'

'After the last half-hour it's probably going to sound stupid,' she hedged, wishing she'd kept her mouth shut.

'Shh!' he said, raising one finger in admonition. 'Tell me.'

'It's just…I need…' she faltered then broke off to drag in a swift breath and force the words out. 'I know we can't have anything more, but could we be friends, Marc? Just…friends, please?'

For several seconds Marc was unable to speak, unable to move as something inside him, some cold hard armour he'd been using to shield his emotions for far too long, suddenly cracked.

She'd been able to tell him just enough, through her tears, for him to feel positively murderous towards the foster-brother who'd tried to destroy her innocence.

It had left her understandably wary, but still she'd risen above it and had the courage to open herself up to other people.

'Ah, Lauren, of course we could,' he murmured softly, certain that she had no idea how difficult he was going to find that. How could she when he'd only just realised it himself?

There she stood, so slender and valiant, completely oblivious to the fact that, even with her face blotchy with the aftermath of her tears, everything about her was a temptation.

Even now the light herbal fragrance of her shampoo drifted towards him, plucking at his nerves and completely overriding the gnawing pain in his leg.

That same scent had lingered tantalisingly in his bathroom for several days after she'd used his shower, or had that just been wishful thinking on his part?

Marc wanted nothing more than to pull her into his arms and... No, that was a lie. He wanted *far* more than that, but as it could never be, he was going to have to settle for what he could have.

For so long he'd steered clear of all but the most cursory contact with people. It was ironic that he should realise just how lonely and isolated he'd become when he'd met the one woman who wouldn't be willing to do anything about it—at least on a long-term basis.

Lauren sighed and turned to retrieve her belongings. 'Time to go home and do a load of laundry, then,' she said quietly. 'I don't suppose I could interest you in an omelette, could I? I don't like to eat until after the classes and then it's too late to have anything heavy.'

He thought of the mountain of work still piled on his desk and balanced it against the prospect of another hour or so in her company. In one direction lay safety and the satisfaction of completing an important task; in the other lay frustration as he fought to resist temptation.

'I've got too much work to do to go home yet, but I could offer you a cup of coffee—decaffeinated.' There was a sharp stab of satisfaction at the brief flash of disappointment when he'd turned down her offer and an equally inappropriate burst of warmth when she smiled up at him.

After this evening, he had no difficulty at all imagining how fiery and tenacious she would be when competing at martial arts. Yet for all that strength there was also a hidden fragility, a vulnerability that she never allowed others to see.

'That would be nice,' she agreed, and turned to follow him out of the physiotherapy department.

He was all too aware of her walking at his side, even though he was having to concentrate on making his strides even. No way was he going to hobble around like an old crock in front of her.

He'd never realised just how intimate his office could be until he shut the door, enclosing the two of them in the evening quiet of his domain. Even his paper-strewn desk took on another dimension when his imagination got to work, especially with Lauren standing beside it.

He turned away quickly to busy his hands with kettle and mugs, desperately searching his mind for a topic of conversation. Otherwise any hope of friendship was doomed.

'Are you an only child?' he blurted, his brain too full of images of Lauren flat on her back across that far too convenient desk to remember if she'd said anything about siblings. Why was this happening to him? He'd never been this adolescent even when he'd *been* an adolescent.

'A very spoiled only child,' she responded with a soft smile. 'Mum said that she'd waited so long for me that she had years of love stored up waiting.'

'She had difficulty conceiving?' he asked idly. Not that he was particularly interested in the medical history of a woman who'd died more than a dozen years ago, but if the conversation meant spending longer in Lauren's company he was willing to talk all night.

Talk all night? Were these the thoughts of the man who preferred to shut himself in his office behind a barricade of ledgers and requisition forms rather than deal with real flesh-and-blood people?

He was so surprised by this constant intrusion of unexpected thoughts that he almost missed what she was saying.

'She couldn't have children at all,' Lauren corrected. 'When she was giving me that mother-daughter puberty talk, she told me that she'd had a burst appendix as a teenager and nearly died of peritonitis. She and Dad had been married for ten years before they went for help. That's when the obs and gyn specialist told her that she'd been left with internal complications that were preventing her conceiving.'

'And in those days there were far fewer options for getting around that sort of problem,' he added understandingly, carefully making sure their fingers didn't touch as he handed her a cup of coffee. He perched on the edge of the desk with his own. 'So they adopted you?'

'Eventually. The trouble was, they would have been that bit older than most couples on the lists and that would have worked against them. In the end, I think they arranged to adopt me privately, otherwise they might have ended up with nothing.'

'Is *that* what they told you?' he demanded, and she realised that he was angry at the thought that she might have been made to feel second best.

'Not at all,' she reassured him hastily. 'That's what I pieced together for myself when I started trying to trace my birth parents. No, I was never left in any doubt that they loved me as much as if I'd been their own from the moment of conception.'

'So, why *did* you want to trace your birth parents? Weren't you afraid you might be hurting your adoptive ones?'

'It was after they'd died,' she explained a little sadly, staring down into her cup. 'I suppose I was hoping that, whatever reason they'd given me away, they might want me back if they knew I had no one of my own left.'

Marc knew only too well what it felt like to lose his entire family, but at least he'd been adult enough to understand the changes in his life and endure them.

How much worse must it be for a child? he wondered. How many other children found themselves in a similar situation to Lauren and decided to search out some family, *any* family, and how many of them were doomed to be rejected all over again?

At least *that* hadn't happened to Lauren. There had probably been more than one obstacle in her way since she'd lost her parents and he could only marvel at how well she'd managed to build a life for herself.

Marc had no idea what drove her to keep moving from job to job the way she had ever since she'd qualified, but he did know that she was a wonderful warm, caring woman who deserved to have a real family of her own.

The mental image of several little carbon copies of Lauren, each with her dark blonde hair and warm honey-coloured eyes, made him smile but the shadowy figure of the man who would be a father to them quickly wiped the smile away again.

Knowing that he could never be that man, responsible for bringing a smile to her face and babies to her arms, left him with a strange hollow ache inside his chest.

He would just have to make the best of what he had. They were already neighbours and colleagues and if this evening was any indication, they could probably become supportive friends. He would only be courting disaster if he set his heart on anything more.

'Time to go home and put a load of washing on,' Lauren said, finally admitting that the last mouthful of coffee she'd been saving as an excuse to prolong their time together was stone cold. 'At least I know that I won't blow my fuse box up this time.'

'It's all working well, is it?' Marc asked as he scooped her folders off the corner of his desk.

She was left with only her handbag and the plastic bag containing her rather noxious uniform to carry as she followed him out into the hallway, pathetically glad of the extra minutes of his company as he accompanied her to her car.

At the last moment, just before she pulled the door shut, he held onto the top of it.

'Do I remember you saying that you were looking forward to doing some fell-walking?' he asked, completely out of the blue.

'You do. That was one of the things that attracted me to the job in Edenthwaite—the chance to get out into open countryside without having to travel for hours to get out of a city.'

'Are you free some time over the weekend? I was

thinking of going out for half a day or so, depending on the weather report.'

Lauren was so surprised by the unexpected suggestion that it took her several seconds to find her tongue.

'I'd love to,' she said hastily in case he took the invitation back. 'Let me look at my diary. I know I'm on early shift on Saturday, so I finish at three, but this late in the year the days are too short for that to be any use.'

She scrabbled hastily through her handbag and found that, as usual, the very thing she wanted had slipped right to the bottom.

'Here it is,' she announced as she dragged the diary out and angled it into the nearby light, flipping pages quickly. 'And I'm off all day Sunday, if that's all right for you?'

'That's perfect, provided the weather co-operates. We're bound to see each other between now and then, but shall we agree to set off mid-morning on Sunday? Do you want to chance finding somewhere *en route* if we get hungry, or would you rather take food with us?'

Suddenly and totally unexpectedly Lauren was beset by doubts.

What was she doing, arranging to spend time with Marc like this? It hadn't seemed quite such a momentous thing to do when he'd suggested going for a walk—the sort of thing that friends would do without a second thought. Why did the fact that Marc had moved the goalposts to include half a day and a shared meal of some sort feel as if their friendly walk had evolved into a date?

The words to call the whole thing off were right

on the tip of her tongue but then she looked up at him.

The light was far from perfect but Lauren couldn't mistake the fact that he really seemed keen for her to agree to his suggestion. It was only a glimpse, but it was almost as if he was reading her mind and was afraid that she was going turn him down after all.

With a conscious resolution to leave her misgivings behind, the decision was made.

'I'll make a bargain with you,' she offered, seeing a way to balance the scales a little. 'If you bring all the necessary safety equipment, I'll take care of the food.' *That* sounded more like two friends going for a walk together, didn't it?

'Accepted with alacrity,' he said with a grin, his teeth very white in spite of the shadows. He stepped back far enough for her to swing her door shut and wished her a safe journey home, then stood for a moment watching while she made her way towards the car-park exit.

Lauren didn't know what made her pause before turning out onto the road. It was probably some juvenile impulse that she'd never had the chance to act on when she'd been a teenager, but suddenly she found herself sitting and watching Marc's reflection in the mirror as he made his way back towards the dark bulk of the hospital.

She was just trying to decide what it was about his height and build that made him so instantly recognisable when she noticed that there was something wrong. It took several seconds before she realised exactly what it was, and if he hadn't reached the door just then she'd have turned the car round to hurry back to him.

'He was limping!' she whispered, suddenly struck by guilt. 'I *knew* I should have insisted that he have an X-ray after I threw him so heavily.'

Reluctantly she put the car in gear and continued her journey home.

'At least he's working in the right place if he needs medical attention,' she consoled herself. 'Mind you, being a man he probably wouldn't even ask for help. He certainly didn't tell *me* he was hurt.'

She was stewing over her part in his injury all the way home and was securing the chain on her door when she finally made her decision.

'I'll wait till he gets home and then I'll check up on him to make sure he's all right.' Otherwise she had a feeling she wasn't going to get much sleep tonight.

CHAPTER EIGHT

'WHAT is it they say about the best-laid plans of mice and men?' Lauren panted crossly as she sprinted towards the hospital's main entrance.

The rain was being driven at her almost horizontally by the bitter wind and she'd completely forgotten to bring her umbrella in her hurry to get here this morning.

She'd had every intention of waiting up until Marc came home last night, but the hour had got later and later so she'd finally been forced to give up and go to bed with the phone placed strategically beside her.

She hadn't realised just how exhausted she must have been by the emotional storm in the physiotherapy department because the next thing she'd known, her alarm had been ringing for the start of another day.

And she'd gone to sleep with the light on, something she never did.

She'd hurried through her early morning routine in the hopes of speaking to him before he set off for the hospital, only to find that she'd missed him.

Either that, or he hadn't come home at all. In which case, was it because of an unexpected disaster at the hospital or because he hadn't been in a fit state to drive himself home?

She'd been so worried that she'd only just stopped herself from phoning Denison and asking if he'd been admitted as a patient overnight. She'd be there soon enough to find out for herself and he wouldn't thank her if it weren't true because the story would be bound to gain embellishment as it went the rounds.

'Well, one place where I can almost guarantee to track him down is in his office,' she muttered under her breath. She barely paused long enough inside the main entrance to shake some of the rain out of her coat and run her fingers through her water-sprinkled hair before she set off up the stairs for the administration department.

'I'm sorry, Lauren, but he left the office about five minutes ago,' said his secretary.

She seemed to be giving Lauren a strange look. Hopefully, that was just because her hair was standing out on end. If it was because Marc now had his leg in plaster, that was another matter.

'If I can't do anything to help, would you like me to give him a message to contact you when he gets back?' she offered helpfully.

'No, thank you, Elaine. I'll try to catch up with him later,' she said with a smile of her own and set off towards her department. Well, it wasn't his secretary's fault she didn't know where he was, and what she wanted to know wasn't something that could be discovered in a relayed message.

'I want to see for myself that he's not limping today,' she muttered as she pressed the button for the lift. 'And if he is, I want him to get someone to give him a once-over even if I have to drag him there myself!'

Luckily, the bell announced the arrival of the lift just as she finished speaking. It wouldn't do her reputation any good if people thought she'd taken to talking to herself.

She would be a few minutes early for her shift but at least that would give her time to dry her hair. It would also give her time to try to control her concern over Marc. It wouldn't be fair to her staff or to their patients if she didn't have her mind on her job.

Marc had finally made the time to visit Lauren's department halfway through the morning, only to find her fully occupied with a frail, elderly patient.

'Shall I do it for you or would you rather do it yourself?' he heard her ask as she wrung out a face-cloth. He didn't need to hear the reply, completely mesmerised by her smile as she gently wiped the delicate, wrinkled skin.

As ward sister she could easily have delegated the task to one of her juniors but he'd already heard her views on just this subject.

'The more experienced a nurse gets, the less actual nursing she seems to do,' she'd complained just last night. 'Each promotion brings more responsibilities but it also brings another mass of paperwork. In the end, we're in danger of becoming administrators rather than nurses, and that's not why I started training...and I've *no* intention of losing out on the contact with patients.'

Well, he thought, drawn closer whether he wanted to or not, she was certainly living up to her intentions if the scene in front of him was anything to go by.

'I expect your transfer took longer than ever, with the weather being so bad,' she was saying.

'It'll be worth it,' he heard the elderly woman reply, her voice stronger than he'd expected in view of the exhaustion evident in her face. 'My Harry couldn't face driving in the city traffic, but he'll be here this afternoon for visiting time.'

'You mean, he hasn't seen you for a week? But that's terrible,' Lauren exclaimed. 'He's going to be so pleased that you're on the mend.'

'Even if I look like a wrung-out dishcloth,' her patient quipped glumly. 'Good job he married me for better or worse.'

'Hmm!' Laura said with a quick glance at her watch. 'We'll have to do something about that. How about if I can get someone to give you a hair-wash? Would that make you feel better?'

'It certainly would!' the woman responded enthusiastically. 'That city hospital was so hot that I nearly melted.'

Marc stepped back out into the corridor, knowing that now wasn't the right time for his conversation with Lauren. He was almost certain that if there wasn't anyone else free, she would wash the elderly lady's hair herself, just because it would give her patient a boost before she saw her husband again. His business would have to wait a little longer.

Still, it was nice to have confirmation that he'd appointed the right member of staff for the position. Now all he had to do was keep his fingers crossed that she would stay more than a few months before she was off to pastures new. The fact that he would also miss her on a personal level wasn't something that he wanted to contemplate.

Lauren glanced at her watch again and felt like growling. So far she'd wasted nearly half of her break trying to track Marc down and she was still no closer.

Perhaps she would do better if she went back to her department and used the phone? It would certainly save time waiting for lifts and energy climbing up and down stairs.

The soft chime of the bell announced the arrival of the lift and she stood to one side so that the occupants could exit easily, but when the doors opened there was only one person in there.

'Marc! I just went to your office, looking for you!' she exclaimed, grateful that her first swift glance had confirmed that at least he wasn't wearing a plaster cast.

'And I just went to *your* domain, looking for you,' he said wryly, bracing one hand against the door to prevent it closing. 'Are we going down or staying up, now that we've found each other?'

Lauren quickly glanced at her watch.

'Perhaps it ought to be down as I'm only on a break,' she decided swiftly, and stepped forward into the pale silvery cubicle. 'We can speak on the way.'

Behind her, the door slid across to shut the two of them in together and Marc reached out to press the appropriate button.

'How are you?' they demanded simultaneously, then laughed.

'Ladies first,' he offered with a smile. 'Tell me how you're feeling today.'

'I'm fine,' she said dismissively. 'I'm far more worried about you. How badly did I hurt you last night?'

'Hurt me?' He looked genuinely puzzled.

'Don't try to fool me because it won't work,' she

said fiercely. 'I saw you in my car mirror last night as I drove away, and you were limping. Did you get someone to check you over?'

He didn't answer for a moment, apparently more interested in something else. She followed the direction of his eyes and found they were both looking at her hand wrapped tightly around his wrist.

Lauren blinked at the sight. She'd been so concerned about Marc that she'd been totally unaware that she'd touched him until that moment. Strangely, although she'd never been a 'toucher', once she'd made the contact, she didn't want to take her hand away.

'Lauren?' Marc murmured as he covered her hand with his own, and she was almost certain that he knew what she'd been thinking. The man saw too much with those smoky grey eyes. But she wasn't going to let him sidetrack her.

'Marc, I was feeling so guilty last night that I waited up for ages to speak to you. In the end, I fell asleep with the light on.'

He gave a brief snort of laughter.

'And *I* didn't sleep properly because, even though I was home so late, your light was still on and I thought you were still too upset to sleep.' He shook his head in disbelief. 'What a comedy of errors!'

'I don't think it's much of a comedy if you were hurt,' she objected. 'Did you need to have X-rays taken?'

'No X-rays. There wasn't time to go to the accident department even if I'd needed to go. When I returned to my office there was—'

'What do you mean, even if you'd needed to go?

Marc, I threw you over my shoulder. You were limping!' she exclaimed.

The bell signalled the lift's arrival at her floor but Lauren was determined to finish the conversation and crossly smacked the button to shut the doors again then pressed another one to travel to the upper floor again.

Marc chuckled out loud at the expression on the faces of the people who had been waiting for the lift. They clearly hadn't been able to believe their eyes when neither Lauren nor Marc had made any attempt to let them enter.

At least she hadn't still been holding his hand at that point. That would *really* have put the cat among the gossiping pigeons.

'Now,' she continued briskly. 'About your limp.'

'Lauren, I'll always have a limp,' he said on a sigh, and shocked her speechless. 'Some days it's worse than others, especially when I'm sent cartwheeling around the floor—as you seem to be doing on a disgustingly regular basis, I might add. But even on a good day it's never going to be a hundred per cent right.'

'Why not? I've certainly not noticed it before. What happened to you? A car accident?' She'd found her voice with a vengeance, the questions tumbling out of her. She'd known him for several weeks now. How could she not have noticed the effects of a permanent injury? Was she so unobservant?

'I suppose you could say it was an accident, of sorts,' he admitted, strangely reluctant. 'It happened when I was in the army.'

'Oh, Marc. Why didn't you tell me? I'd never have agreed to use you for my demonstrations if I'd known. I'm so sorry.' A sudden thought struck her. 'Are you sure you ought to go fell-walking on Sunday? Won't that cause a problem?'

'Walking is good for me, so you're not using me as an excuse to wimp out,' he objected. 'Anyway, you promised to feed me and I'm holding you to it.'

'Are you sure?' she demanded, not really certain whether she wanted him to cancel the outing to allow his leg time to calm down or confirm it so that they could spend at least part of the day together.

What was the matter with her? Was this mental confusion a taste of what she'd missed out on when she'd been a teenager?

'Lauren, I'm sure,' he said firmly, and his conviction was clear even though the bell was intruding to tell them that the lift had arrived on the ground floor. 'I'll see you on Sunday if I don't see you… Oh, Lord, where's my brain?' he demanded suddenly and turned to get into the lift again.

He pressed the button to send the lift down once more, totally ignoring the woman who called from the other side of the hallway and started rushing towards the lift, obviously hoping to get in with them.

'There was another reason why I needed to see you,' Marc continued obliviously as the door slid swiftly closed. 'The same reason why I was kept late in my office last night, actually.'

Lauren couldn't help it. She was convulsed with sudden laughter at the sight of the poor woman's face.

'Oh, dear. Marc, I do hope you're prepared for your character to be shredded.' She chuckled. 'That's the second time we've ignored other would-be passengers. The tale's going to be all over the hospital within the hour.'

'If people haven't anything better to talk about,' he said with a dismissive one-shouldered shrug. 'As I was saying, I had a visitor last night, one of the local policemen.'

'And?' She frowned, not understanding what it could have to do with her.

'And he had received a formal complaint that Laurel Wainwright, who is apparently passing herself off as Lauren Scott and working at Denison Memorial as a qualified nurse when she's nothing of the sort, took a very expensive car without the owner's consent.'

'What?' Lauren gasped in shock then groaned. 'Not again! Who made the complaint this time, and whose car am I supposed to have stolen?'

'The complaint was made by someone called Robert Wainwright and he claims to be your father.'

Lauren's jaw dropped in amazement. She wasn't sure which surprised her more, that this unknown man—probably the same one who'd been behind all her recent troubles—was claiming to be her father, or that he would actually accuse his supposed daughter of stealing his car.

The one thing she still had no idea about was why he was doing any of it at all, especially as it was so easy to disprove. She was not—neither had she ever been—called Laurel Wainwright, and far from being Robert Wainwright, owner of an expensive car, her father had been dead for a long time.

This time, when the lift stopped, Marc took her elbow and started to lead the way towards his office.

Suddenly realising where they were going, Lauren stopped in her tracks.

'Marc, no! I've got to get to the ward. It's nearly visiting time and I need to be there in case any of the relatives have any questions.'

'Don't worry, You've another quarter of an hour to go yet. Anyway, I can phone the ward from the office and let them know you've been delayed by an administrative problem.'

'That's not fair on my juniors,' she objected. 'Apart from the visitors, there are a couple of very demanding patients on the ward at the moment. Everyone seems to be desperate to get well in time to be home for Christmas. Do you realise, it's only about eight weeks away?'

'I don't even want to think about that yet.' It was Marc's turn to groan. 'There's that staff social-fundraiser thing to finish organising before then, and the flu season will probably have started, too, so we'll be overflowing with patients and short of staff.'

Lauren smiled absently at Elaine as Marc tried to march her past his secretary's desk, only to be halted by a small sheaf of messages.

'You'll want to look at the top one,' she said pointedly.

He glanced quickly at it and gave a pleased grunt. 'Good work, Elaine. I'll get straight back to him,' he said, and then he was in motion again.

'Take a seat,' he said to Lauren as he reached for the phone, not even waiting long enough for her to close the door.

'Yes, sir!' she muttered under her breath and saw from the sharp look he sent her that he'd heard what she'd said. Well, she thought slightly defensively, it *had* sounded suspiciously like an order. Perhaps it was another lingering effect of his time in the armed forces.

And what *had* he done when he was still part of the military? she wondered, her eyes running over him as he settled himself in his high-backed chair and waited for the call to be answered. She couldn't really see him as an infantryman, his face camouflaged with random splodges and stripes of green and brown while he ran around carrying weapons. But in spite of his present job, neither did he strike her as a man who would be content with a life spent entirely behind a desk. His body was far too fit and well muscled for that.

In fact, the more she came to know Marc, the more convinced she became that there were great hidden depths to him. He certainly wasn't a one-dimensional person.

It was just her luck, really. She'd always known that there was no point in wishing for the moon and she'd long grown accustomed to the idea that her job and the pleasure she took in doing it well was going to have to be her focus.

Then she'd moved to Edenthwaite and met Marc, and in spite of their uncomfortable and sometimes downright confrontational beginnings, she was all too aware that, if things had been different, he might have been the perfect man to complete her life.

Lauren allowed herself a brief fantasy, trying to imagine how this scene would play itself out if the two of them had a normal man-woman relationship.

Would she be bold enough to sit on the edge of the desk to be nearer to him? If she were to give him admiring glances, would he return them? And when he finished his call, would he take the opportunity for an illicit touch of intimacy? A kiss or two, perhaps?

Her eyes strayed upward, admiring the lips that had actually ravished hers for several exquisite moments last night.

Without memories of teenage experimentation to fall back on, she'd never realised just how strong her reaction would be to a man's kiss. Had it just been the novelty of the situation? If he were to do it again, would her reaction be the same? She was too inexperienced to know.

Her gaze slid upward over the lean planes of his face and finally reached those fascinating smoky grey eyes, only to find that they were watching her with an uncomfortably knowing expression even as he conducted his conversation.

'Well, thank you very much for that,' he was saying as she tried to gather her composure, her eyes now firmly fixed on her clenched hands. 'I'll hear from you when you get some more results to your enquiries.' He was silent for a moment, obviously listening, then laughed. 'Yes, I'm sure Lauren will be relieved to know that you're not going to be arresting her, too. Many thanks for getting back to me so quickly.'

Lauren was sitting wide-eyed when Marc put the phone down, her embarrassment at being caught eyeing him up totally forgotten.

'Arresting me?' she squeaked, suddenly realising that he must have been speaking to the police. 'What for? I haven't done anything. You've already checked my credentials.'

'He knows that now, too. That's why he's confirmed that there would be no grounds for arresting you,' Marc said, irritatingly patiently, and Lauren suddenly realised just how much his attitude towards her had changed from the first time they'd met in this room. Far from being confrontational, he actually seemed to be on her side now, even though he hadn't yet given her any of the details of his conversations with the police.

'So, are you going to explain what's been going on, or will I have to throw you around a bit first?' she threatened, putting on a fierce expression, her heart inexplicably light in spite of the situation.

'No! Not that! I'll tell you,' he exclaimed, responding briefly to her attempt at humour before he sobered. 'As you've probably gathered, that was the policeman I spoke to last night—the one who was investigating the allegation of theft of a rather desirable Jaguar car.'

'A Jaguar?' She laughed aloud. 'I've never even sat in one, let alone stolen it. I take it this Laurel Wainwright, if she exists, comes from a wealthy family?'

'She exists and it would appear so,' he confirmed. 'According to her father, she's been a bit unstable and highly strung ever since she was a child and as she's grown up the problem has grown with her. Apparently it's blossomed into paranoia and an overwhelming persecution complex, despite the fact he and his wife have done everything they could to give her a perfect life.'

'She sounds like a real sweetheart, but how on earth did they get the two of us mixed up? Surely they must have made some preliminary enquiries before they started rubbishing *my* character?'

'Apparently they did,' he said. 'They hired a private investigator to track her down and he found you here.'

'But, Marc, nothing about this Laurel sounds the least bit like me. Oh, I admit there's only one letter separating our first names, but as for the rest... Surely the parents must have given the man a photo of their daughter. Then it would be easy for him to see that he'd got the wrong person.'

'*That* is part of the problem,' he admitted, leaning forward to slide a piece of paper across the desk towards her. 'This is a faxed copy of the photo he used to identify you.'

Lauren picked it up, expecting to need nothing more than a cursory glance to prove that the man she'd thrown over her shoulder that first night in the car park had deserved every bit of her swift reaction. What she saw robbed her of speech and thought as she stared in disbelief.

'Marc!' she gasped after several long seconds. 'This is... It looks... *She* looks just like me.'

'I know,' he said softly, suddenly standing right beside her as though he wanted to be prepared for any reaction, as though he cared. 'Anyone can see that the similarities are quite uncanny.'

'No. You don't understand,' she said, strange, turbulent emotions starting to build up inside her as she stared long and hard at the picture, carefully cataloguing points that only she would notice. 'She's the same as me, but *only* to me,' she said, then gave a huff of frustration when the words clearly didn't convey what she wanted them to. Then she had a flash of inspiration.

'Where's the nearest mirror?' she demanded, then

remembered the one tucked in the inside pocket of her bag. 'Here. Look in the mirror and describe what you see, concentrating on the differences between one side of your face and the other. For example, when you grin, does one corner of your mouth lift further than the other and, if so, which one is it?'

Marc frowned but obviously decided to humour her as he turned his head from one side to the other to look for any dissimilarities.

'You mean, like the fact that I've got a chickenpox scar just in front of my left ear and another one high up under my hair on my forehead?' He pointed to each in turn.

'Exactly those sorts of things,' she agreed in delight. This was going to be easy. 'So there's one scar by your ear on the left and the other on your forehead on the right, but where are they when you look in the mirror?'

'That's easy. My reflection isn't called a mirror image for nothing,' he said. 'They're apparently in front of my right ear and the left side of my forehead.'

'Now look at this photo and tell me what you can see—apart from the obvious difference in hair lengths, that is.'

Lauren pinned a similar smile on her face to the one in the picture and held it up beside her face, waiting impatiently while Marc took his time looking from picture to person and back again.

'Good Lord, I see what you mean!' he exclaimed suddenly. 'You've got a slight dimple in your right cheek and the hair in that little widow's peak at the front of your hair angles the other way, too. She's got exactly the same, but the other way round... Ah, but what if it's just the fact that the picture's been printed with the negative reversed?' he suggested on a sudden inspiration. 'That would easily explain the differences.'

'With that row of cars in the background of the picture all with their number plates the right way round? I don't think so,' she pointed out triumphantly, barely allowing herself to think about the obvious conclusion hovering at the end of this. She couldn't allow herself to think it because she knew it couldn't be true, and yet…

'Well, if this is the real Laurel Wainwright, I can see why that investigator was confused,' Marc said with a disbelieving shake of his head. 'You look like identical twins.'

'Except we can't be,' Lauren said, falling back on what she'd always known to be true. 'My parents never made any secret about the fact that I was adopted and they would certainly have said something if I'd been a twin.'

Marc looked thoughtful. 'I expect you're right as far as that goes, but what if *they* didn't know? Just in case there's something to it, I hope you won't mind if I pass the information on to the local police. Perhaps they can use it to eliminate you from the equation once and for all—especially that bit about the mirror images. Maybe that will get Robert Wainwright to call his investigator off you and leave you alone.'

His phone rang and Lauren suddenly remembered that Marc hadn't contacted the ward to warn them that she might be late. Her colleague was *not* going to be a very happy lady.

Itching to be on her way, Lauren was glad the call was a short one.

'Where were we?' Marc said.

'I don't know where you are or what you're going to do, but I'm off to my ward—now,' Lauren said as she briskly straightened out of her seat. 'I've just remembered that we didn't let the staff know that I was going to be late. I'd be very grateful if you'd phone and let them know I'm on my way, just in case someone's waiting to speak to me.'

She took the stairs, telling herself that she was in too much of a hurry to wait for the lift. She was unwilling to admit that it would probably be several days before she wanted to get into it again. That confined space would be far too full of memories for comfort.

Anyway, if she stayed as far away from it as possible there would be less chance of jogging people's memories. So far, she'd managed to avoid being the subject of any juicy titbits on the hospital grapevine. Unfortunately, that probably wasn't the case any more.

She knew what fertile ground hospital grapevines could live in from her previous posts. She was going to have to wait and see just how lurid the tales became. She certainly hadn't intended doing anything that would make her the centre of attention.

'Oh, I needed this,' Lauren groaned as they reached the top of the first stiff climb. She sank to the tightly nibbled turf regardless of how wet or dry it was and stared up at the pale china-blue wintry sky.

'It's been a rough week,' Marc agreed as he

sprawled out beside her, his well-worn rucksack acting as a backrest. 'Has it started easing off a bit?'

'Not so you'd notice,' she grumbled, hoping he would think the colour in her cheeks was the result of the bracing wind. She would never have believed how explicit some of the stories had become. She'd barely *heard* of some of the things people had been talking about, let alone done them in a hospital lift.

'Elaine has been keeping me up to date with some of the more…*colourful* tales, otherwise I'm pretty well insulated from them in my office.'

'Lucky you! It couldn't possibly be that you're in a position of power and people don't want to upset you, could it?' she asked sweetly. 'You wouldn't believe some of the things I'm being asked, and by complete strangers, too.'

He chuckled and she knew he had seen her deepening blush. 'That bad, were they?' he asked with an unexpectedly salacious wink. 'Are you going to tell me what we've been up to?'

'I am *not*,' she said firmly, then couldn't help responding to his wicked grin with a chuckle of her own. He was certainly helping her to see the funny side of the situation.

Suddenly she was more glad then ever that she'd agreed to come out fell-walking with him today in spite of her reservations. She couldn't remember when she'd ever felt this light-hearted before.

'Anyway,' she added daringly, 'half of the suggestions probably aren't physically possible, unless one or both of us is double-jointed.'

His eyes widened for a second, almost as if she'd shocked him, but then his hearty laughter was echoing off the surrounding hills.

*   *   *

The biting wind had dropped but the fine bright day had degenerated into a bone-chilling mist in the middle of the afternoon.

Much as she hated to see the day end, Lauren had to agree with Marc that it would be safer to make for home. The last thing they needed was to become disorientated in such an unforgiving environment. A night on the Cumbrian fells at this time of year wouldn't be a joke, even with someone as solidly reassuring as Marc at her side.

They'd reached the start of the last downhill stretch that would take them back to Marc's car when she first heard the distant call.

'I'm glad I'm not a sheep on a day like this,' she commented, grateful for the quality of the weather-proof clothing she'd bought soon after arriving in Edenthwaite. She shuddered again at the thought of having to spend the night out in such inclement weather even with a sheep's thick woolly coat on.

She heard the sound again, weak and thready, as it was bounced around them by the echoes.

'Listen to that poor animal, Marc. Don't you feel sorry for it, being left up on these hills at this time of year?'

Without warning he stopped in his tracks. 'There's something wrong, Lauren. That can't be a sheep because they've all been brought down to the lower pastures by now. The hill farmers always do it before the bad weather comes because the ewes are already pregnant with next year's crop of spring lambs.'

He turned around in a circle, his grey eyes almost matching the colour of the drizzle-dampened limestone boulders around them as he scanned their surroundings.

'Hel-lo!' he called suddenly, startling Lauren. 'Is anybody there?' The echoes had barely died away when she heard that strange bleating noise again. She didn't know whether it was because of Marc's conviction, but this time it really did sound more human.

'Where are you?' Marc called again, then waited for the cry to come again before he tried once more to pinpoint the direction it was coming from.

'Keep calling!' he instructed as he set off at an angle from their original route taking them well away from the safe pathway they'd been following.

Lauren made certain to follow close behind. She had both compass and a large-scale map of the area in the big square pocket on the front of her cagoule, but she didn't want to have to find her own way if she could help it.

It took nearly half an hour to reach the couple trapped in an almost hidden gully.

'Thank God you found us,' the young woman babbled over and over again, obviously close to the end of her endurance as she rocked backwards and forwards with her arms wrapped awkwardly around herself for warmth.

Both were completely soaked to the skin but Lauren had a nasty feeling that was the least of their problems.

Her companion was ominously silent, his face pale grey in the sullen light and wet with a mixture of mist and sweat.

'Jason's broken his ankle,' the young woman announced suddenly, her eyes almost feverishly bright for a moment. 'He was climbing up the slope to see if he could see the way back to the car and everything was wet. When he slipped his foot got caught between two boulders and twisted.' She looked up at Lauren. 'I heard it snap,' she whispered, looking very much as if she was going to be sick.

While she'd been talking Marc had slipped his rucksack off, grabbing two space-age foil survival blankets from one of the pockets. He handed one to Lauren to wrap around the woman before he knelt down beside the young man to do the same, his manner very professional as he quickly checked the vital signs.

Lauren was expecting to have to take over for the more detailed examination of the man's injuries but Marc paused only long enough to call over his shoulder.

'Lauren, could you get the medical kit out of my rucksack? It'll be right at the bottom.'

She hurried to locate it, fully prepared to find one of the compact kits specially designed for basic amateur first aid. What she found was a very professional-looking waterproof case that was obviously far too swish to be equipped with just a triangular bandage and a packet of plasters to cover the odd blister.

Was this the sort of thing he'd had to carry when he'd been in the army? she wondered as she followed his directions to open the case. She nearly swallowed her tongue when she saw the array of supplies neatly stacked inside. She'd heard of Third World hospitals that weren't as well equipped.

'It's a bad break,' he muttered as he leant closer to her, knowing it was something that neither of the young couple needed to hear at this moment. Not that they would be able to hear much over the young man's increasingly agonised moans, but it was hard for him to keep the injured ankle still when he was still shivering so hard.

'I'm going to need to splint it before we can move him,' Marc continued aloud as he reached for a slender strip of rigid plastic tucked down one side of the kit.

'Lauren, can you grab those Velcro strips ready to strap his legs together?' he asked as he flipped up a partition in the other side to reveal a miniature pharmacy complete with disposable syringes and needles.

Lauren was speechless as she watched the smooth skill with which he drew up fluid from an all-too-familiar little glass bottle and prepared to inject it into the young man at his side.

'What are you *doing*?' she whispered urgently, grabbing hold of his wrist to stop him giving the injection. 'That's morphine!'

'Of course it is,' he hissed back. 'You don't think I'd try splinting the poor beggar's ankle without it, do you? He's in enough pain as it is.'

'But you shouldn't be walking around with that stuff in your rucksack. It's a class A drug,' she said in horror, wondering how on earth a hospital administrator came to have it in his possession in the first place. It was definitely hospital issue, from the look of the container. He couldn't have misappropriated it from the hospital, could he?

'Lauren, it's all right,' he said as he gave her hand a brief reassuring squeeze, almost as though he were reading her mind. 'I *am* qualified to do this. It's what I did in the army.'

CHAPTER NINE

ALTHOUGH it was still early evening, it was completely dark by the time Marc finally pulled into his driveway and switched off the engine.

He rested his head back against the seat and turned to look at the tousle-headed woman in the seat next to him.

'Thank you for coming with me, today, Lauren,' he said quietly. 'In spite of the unexpected excitement, I don't remember when I've enjoyed a day more.'

Suddenly there was so much more he wished he could say but, because he was the man he was and she was a woman who never put down roots, they were obviously fated to go as far as friendship and no further.

When had that prospect started to become a disappointment rather than a relief?

He could admit, now, that Lauren had somehow managed to get under his skin right from the first time he'd set eyes on her, but because he'd known she wouldn't be staying in Edenthwaite long, he'd thought it wouldn't be a problem. He wasn't in the market for a relationship, anyway.

Now he found his admiration for her growing with each new facet of her character that he discovered. Now she wasn't just a good-looking woman who'd somehow managed to remind his body what hormones were for, she was someone he'd come to care for, too.

'I must admit, things got a bit hairy when you took off to alert the rescue services,' she said. 'Mina was convinced you'd never be able to find us again and started to panic.'

That had been about the time he'd been cursing himself up hill and down dale for selfishly leaving his mobile phone at home. He'd been so determined that nothing was going to intrude on his time with Lauren that he'd totally ignored the instrument's potential usefulness.

He'd been rewarded with having to do nearly two miles of running on a less than willing leg before he'd been able to contact the rescue services, then a chilly delay while he'd waited to guide them back up to the victims. If his leg played up tomorrow he only had himself to blame.

At least Jason and Mina would be safely tucked up in bed soon, both of them having been transported to the city hospital where Jason's fractures would probably have to be pinned and plated. He definitely stood a better chance of a full recovery than he would have if he'd spent the night out in the open. He would probably never know exactly how close he'd come to losing his leg, or even his life.

'In spite of all the drama, it was a wonderful day,' she agreed, breaking into his thoughts with a smile that sent a swift shaft of heat right through him. 'In fact, it's been so good that I don't want it to end yet.'

'Well, it's not late, so is there any particular reason why it should?' he heard himself say, and only just suppressed a groan. Was he a masochist, wanting to spend even more time with Lauren? And this time in the close confines of a tiny cottage.

Marc knew he needed to talk to her—to explain something beyond his simple statement that he was qualified to administer morphine—but he was dreading it because he knew the explanations couldn't stop there.

Everything had been so much simpler when he'd managed to convince himself that they would just be two colleagues from Denison Memorial out for a walk in the Cumbrian fells.

Except even *that* innocuous occupation hadn't been quite that simple or that innocent, at least as far as he was concerned.

All day he'd been watching her lithe, slender body striding out beside him. He'd listened to her thoughts and debated her ideas on almost every subject under the sun and, best of all, he'd joined in with her laughter.

Sometimes it felt as if a lifetime had gone by since he'd been able to laugh like that; aeons that he'd been living with the guilt that had beaten him down so that it seemed as if there was no laughter left in him.

A tiny voice in a corner of his mind was trying to tempt him to keep silent, not to risk the tentative bonds they were forming by telling her too much about himself, but honesty was ingrained too deeply for him to take the easy way out.

Even though their relationship could never progress much further—certainly not to the ultimate— he already cared too much for her to contemplate trying to hide who he was and what he'd done.

'I'm feeling a bit guilty about accepting your hospitality again,' she said with an almost impish glint in her eyes. 'It *should* be my turn to play host, but you've restored that gorgeous fireplace in your cottage, so yours feels so much more cosy than mine.'

'Well, then, bring your guilt in with you and we'll see if we can roast it into submission in front of a few logs,' he invited with a chuckle.

Marc grabbed his rucksack and Lauren took charge of the heavy-duty plastic bag into which they'd dumped their muddy walking boots.

'Are you ready for a cup of tea?' he asked, fully aware that he was putting off the evil moment just a little longer. If she reacted badly to his revelations, these might be the last good memories he shared with her.

'I could murder a cup!' Lauren exclaimed, her voice temporarily muffled as she pulled her cagoule off over her head.

When he saw the old gold strands of her hair standing on end he had to smile and, without stopping to consider what he was doing, he found himself reaching out to run his fingers gently over her head to smooth them down.

There were several seconds of almost electric silence while she gazed up at him, and he froze, wondering just for a moment whether he'd overstepped the bounds. Then she smiled at him, softly, almost shyly, and reached up to cover his hand briefly with her own, and he realised that she'd taken another giant step forward.

'That's nice,' she said, then bit her lip. He could almost hear the conflict going on inside her head as she tried to find the words she wanted, and it mattered enough to him to wait patiently until she found them.

'I don't have any problem with nursing the patients, but for years I've preferred to keep a deliberate gap between myself and the rest of the world.'

She met his eyes deliberately as though trying to gauge his response. He hoped she could see that he understood. He'd had very different reasons for putting distance between himself and the rest of the world but the results had ultimately been the same.

'With you, it's different,' she said suddenly, now seeming to avoid meeting his eyes. 'It doesn't feel as if you're invading my space so much as…as *sharing* it. And when you touch me…my elbow, my back, my hair…it feels almost as if you care.'

Marc could only guess just how much courage it had taken for her to say so much, to let him inside her thoughts and feelings like that, and his heart swelled with a feeling strangely like pride.

'If it feels as if I care,' he began in a suddenly husky voice, 'then it's because I *do* care, probably more than you realise.'

And much more than he'd been prepared to admit, even to himself, he added silently, suddenly afraid that the ordered world he'd built for himself had been wrenched out of his control while he hadn't been looking.

With or without his permission, his emotions had slipped the restraints he'd put on them. He already cared for Lauren more than he'd ever thought his battered heart would dare.

He glanced uneasily towards the fireplace, filled with a growing sense of panic when he realised he'd probably reached the point of no return.

Still, he found himself grasping at the chance for a reprieve and when he noticed that the fire would need lighting again, he stepped back out of reach.

'If you'd put the kettle on, then I'll get that fire going. How do you feel about making toast in front of it when it's properly alight?'

'I haven't done that for donkey's years!' She laughed, clearly delighted with the idea. 'Have you got one of those long-handled forks so we don't burn our hands?'

'Two of them. I'll get them out,' he promised, and went to bring in another armful of logs and some kindling. They could kneel in front of the fire while they made the toast and then graduate to more comfortable seats when the time for their conversation arrived.

Half an hour later Marc's sides were already aching so much that he could hardly draw a full breath.

'I've never known anyone who could burn so much toast,' he wheezed, and couldn't help chuckling anew at the glare Lauren threw him.

'It's not my fault if the bread keeps falling off the fork,' she complained. 'I was only trying to turn it round to get it evenly browned all over.'

'And then had to fish it out of the fire…how many times?' he challenged.

Lauren glowered again and pretended to threaten him with the business end of the long-handled fork. 'Well, I didn't really have room for that last piece, anyway. I'm completely full.'

She leaned back against the thick upholstery of his reclining chair, her sock-covered feet stretched out beside his much longer ones towards the flickering flames licking their way around the edges of the logs.

He'd only switched on the small table lamp the other side of his reclining chair, the blazing logs providing all the illumination they'd needed for their task. Now he turned just far enough to be able to watch her without being obvious, imprinting in his memory the sight of her face, gilded by the firelight, her hair, more spun gold than old gold in this light, and her eyes, as warm and glowing as any fine whisky. It was her smile, though, that he wanted to remember most clearly, half-afraid that once he'd told her his failings he'd never see it again.

As if she was tuned directly into the train of his thoughts she turned and looked straight into his eyes.

'Tell me about what happened to you in the army,' she asked simply, then added firmly, 'Everything that happened.' And he knew his time had finally run out. It was time to pay the piper.

'I was a doctor,' Marc began after a tense moment, his tone almost challenging her to comment.

Lauren almost did, but then she remembered the way he'd waited so patiently for her to find the words she'd needed when it had been her turn, and she managed to bite her tongue in time to stay silent.

As if her silence gave him permission to speak, he continued.

'It was all I'd ever wanted to be, but there wasn't a hope that my parents would be able to pay towards my training. My father was a chronic bronchitic who developed heart problems that prevented him doing much of anything, let alone work. Mum had to do so much for him that the only work she felt happy about taking was as a part-time cleaner going round the city offices at night when Dad was asleep. At least I was there to fetch things for him if he woke up.'

Lauren's heart ached for the boy he'd been. It didn't sound as if it had been much of a childhood. At least she'd had her parents until she'd been fourteen. Her problems hadn't started until *after* they'd died.

'I left school as soon as it was legal so that Mum could spend some time with Dad when she wasn't exhausted, but that summer he had a fatal heart attack.'

'Oh, Marc,' she murmured before she could stop herself. She could only imagine how devastated he must have been that his help had come too late for the two of them to enjoy it for very long.

Suddenly Lauren was struck by the urge to form some sort of tangible bond between them and before she could reason herself out of the idea threw caution to the winds and threaded her fingers through his where his hand lay on the fireside rug between them.

He'd been staring blindly at the fire while he'd been speaking but at her touch turned pain-filled eyes towards her. He was still for a timeless moment before he tightened his fingers and dredged up a small smile of appreciation, and Lauren realised that it meant more to her than any expensive gift could have.

'I worked my heart out that summer, probably so I didn't have time to think about everything I'd lost, but when school opened again, Mum informed me that I was going back so I could get the exams to get into medical school.' He shook his head and gave a wry grin. 'I'd be the first one to admit that I'm stubborn but she could have given the world lessons in obstinate. Needless to say, the beginning of September saw me sitting in a classroom again but she didn't get things all her own way. I wasn't going to let her work herself into the grave supporting me, so I approached the army about sponsoring me through medical school.'

'And once you qualified you stayed as an army medic until you were injured?'

'In essence, yes, but it wasn't quite as simple as that.' He was silent, almost as if he was having to steel himself for the next part of the story, and Lauren felt an unknown dread begin to seize her.

'I married Erica right after I qualified,' he continued, his words apparently cold and unemotional, but they struck Lauren like a physical blow, leaving her feeling strangely sick and disorientated. 'I had my first foreign posting just after Heather was born and though I wanted the two of them to stay safe in England, Erica was determined to take advantage of the chance to travel.'

He paused to run the fingers of his free hand through his hair and Laurel could see from the visible tremor in them that he wasn't nearly as composed as he appeared.

She could feel his tension in the fingers entwined with hers and for his sake forced herself to ignore the surge of jealousy that had filled her when she'd learned he'd had a child.

'You probably remember a few years ago that there was a time when military bases were being targeted by terrorist groups—rocket launchers being used against surveillance posts, car bombs and so on.'

Lauren nodded silently, remembering the shocking images on the news.

'Of course, that meant safety restrictions, so Erica wasn't free to get about the way she wanted. She wasn't happy about it—said there wasn't much point being abroad if she only saw the same four walls all the time.'

Lauren didn't really want to hear the details, but Marc definitely needed to tell her.

'That morning we had a dreadful row,' he continued in a raw voice. 'I'd only just come off duty, late as usual. Heather was teething so Erica had been up and stewing for hours. She said she couldn't stand being cooped up any longer and wanted me to drive her car out to the airport so she could get the first plane home.

'I wanted her to wait until I'd had some sleep and then we'd sit down and talk about it but she exploded. Heather was screaming as she carried her out to her car, and I suddenly realised that she'd already packed their things. I ran out to plead with her…at least not to drive while she was so angry.'

Marc was obviously trying to recount the sequence of events in as unemotional a way as possible but it wasn't really working. The tremor had spread to his voice now, and she couldn't imagine the pictures he was seeing inside his head.

'I don't know whether she just wasn't concentrating, or what, but instead of putting the car into reverse to take it out of the driveway, she must have put it into first gear. Then she put her foot down, hard, and crashed straight into the house. They said that she and Heather died almost instantly.'

The last words had emerged as a faint whisper and

she was stunned to see that there were tears trickling steadily down his cheeks.

For one dreadful moment she was paralysed by self-doubt.

If he'd been a patient she'd have had no hesitation in wrapping a comforting arm around his shoulders for a while until he had time to regain control, before offering a cup of tea. But this was Marc, and for some reason his unhappiness affected her far more personally than anything since the death of her own parents.

And in the end that was the key.

The way she felt about Marc, how could she not take him in her arms and cradle his head against her with a stroking hand? How could she not feel her own heart aching when his sobs suddenly erupted, almost as if this was the first time he'd really allowed himself to grieve for his wife and child?

She rocked him gently, time unimportant as she alternately stroked his back and ran her fingers soothingly through the silky strands of his hair.

Finally he subsided into silence and this time it was her turn to offer the freshly pressed handkerchief, only in her case it was a small handful of paper tissues.

She waited a moment while he mopped the tear-stains from his face before she asked the question burning on the tip of her tongue.

'But, Marc, I still don't understand why you stopped practising medicine.'

'Isn't it obvious?' he demanded thickly, clearly uncomfortable with his loss of control and unwilling to meet her eyes. 'If it hadn't been for me and my career, they'd never have died. I was supposed to save lives, that was my job, but I couldn't save my own wife and daughter. If I couldn't do that, how could I trust myself with the responsibility of other peoples' lives?'

She supposed there was some sort of skewed logic in it but the conclusion he'd drawn wasn't really rational.

'So you made the decision there and then?' she asked in disbelief. 'While you were standing there surrounded by all that carnage and probably in deep shock? Did no one question it? I expect the medical corps is slightly different to most army units, but didn't any of your superior officers talk to you about what you were doing and why?'

'Not until I came out of hospital and by that time it didn't matter what they said, I'd already signed all the necessary papers.'

'By the time you came out of hospital?' she repeated incredulously. 'What was the matter with you?'

He shrugged. 'I was in front of the car when she put her foot down and drove straight at me. I ended up underneath it, then several tons of rubble landed on top of it. There isn't quite enough metalwork in my legs to set off airport sensors but it might cause a problem if I'm cremated.'

Lauren was shocked into silence, needing a moment to get everything straight in her head before she spoke again. Unfortunately, the longer she thought about it the more outraged she became and it was going to be hard to keep that out of her voice if she didn't speak soon.

'I won't bother to tell you that you're crazy if you feel guilty—you've probably been told more than once before that she was an adult and made her own choices. But as for you…do you mean to tell me that you decided that day that the career you'd wanted since you were a child—the only career you'd ever wanted—was over? I can't believe that you didn't enjoy it any more, that there was no challenge in it, no satisfaction in being able to help someone helpless and in pain? I can tell you, that wasn't what it looked like to me today.'

For just a second there was an expression of betrayal in his eyes and Lauren was certain that she'd just completely alienated him with her sharp tongue.

The thought that he might resent her for what she'd said and break off their fledgling friendship was heart-breaking, especially as she was only just realising how much her heart had become involved.

But she couldn't in all honesty have spoken anything but the truth as she saw it.

Then his expression changed, became more sombre and thoughtful, and she began to hope that all was not completely lost.

'You're right about today. I *did* enjoy the challenge,' he admitted with a sharp sigh. 'In spite of the conditions and the lack of equipment and so on, I actually felt alive for the first time in a long time.'

'I bet that feeling beats shuffling papers into a cocked hat,' she teased, surprised to find that their hands were still entwined.

'You'd win,' he sighed again, and this one sounded as if it came all the way from his soul. 'I've missed it so much and can't believe what a fool I've been, to make such an enormous decision in that way.'

'It was probably partly compounded by your stay

in hospital,' she guessed. 'I expect most people were too shocked to know what to say to you, so didn't dare come and visit. That meant you had far too much time on your hands to brood about what you'd lost, and thinking that if only you could have done such and such, then it wouldn't have happened.'

'You're right again,' he admitted grimly. 'And once my decision to resign my commission was made common knowledge, it was almost as if I'd ceased to exist for them; as if I'd died, too.'

'And that would have been like yet another bereavement,' she murmured softly when she realised that he'd also lost all contact with the wider 'family' of his military colleagues.

Marc groaned and let his head drop back against the edge of the seat behind them. 'It's all so pathetically obvious when you look at it like that,' he said. 'If only I'd met you years ago, you could have beaten some sense into my thick head.' He brought their joined hands up to his mouth and pressed a kiss to her knuckles.

Lauren watched in bemusement, wondering how different *her* life would have been by now if she'd met Marc earlier.

Since she'd moved to Edenthwaite her life and her attitude to it had changed so much that she still hadn't got her bearings. And things were still changing.

She wasn't the same woman who'd moved from job to job, knowing that something was missing from her life. She certainly wouldn't have had the courage to sit in front of a fire holding a man's hand, let alone cradle him in her arms. And as for the dreams she'd started having—dreams that went far beyond the reality of her limited experience—where once they would almost have terrified her, they now only made her long to see if her imagination could possibly hold a candle to reality.

He lifted his head to meet her eyes and in the space of one tantalising, terrifying moment she knew that he was going to kiss her again, and for the first time in her life she knew what it felt like to really want it to happen.

Deep inside, nerves and muscles clenched and quivered in anticipation of the pleasure to come. It almost felt as though the whole world held its breath with her while she waited for him to come closer, his smoke-grey eyes darkening to slate as they focused on her mouth.

And then he was releasing her, not just straightening away from her but rising all the way to his feet. For several seconds he towered over her, almost as if he was regretting his decision. She gazed helplessly up the long powerful length of his body, unable to understand the reason he'd changed his mind.

'You'll need to catch up on your sleep after the day you've had today,' he said, long after the silence in the room had grown uncomfortable. He even hesitated before he offered his hand to help her to her feet and Lauren's short-lived happiness faded several more shades.

Why was he behaving like this? she wondered, standing woodenly while he fetched her cagoule. Was it because of the way she'd reacted the first time he'd kissed her, or did it have more to do with his changed opinion of her since she'd harangued him over his crazy self-destructive decision to give up medicine? Would she ever know?

Gentleman to the end, he actually escorted her right to her door before he said goodnight, and she could see his outline through the frosted glass panel, waiting until he heard her slip the safety chain into position.

'Gentlemen with nice manners are all very well,' she muttered as she climbed the stairs to her solitary bed. 'But when the woman in question is so inexperienced that she has no idea how to tell him that she would welcome his advances...' She threw up her hands with a growl of disgust, knowing she sounded positively Victorian.

It wasn't until she was lying in bed that she remembered several odd snatches of conversation they'd had during their wonderful walk and began to wonder if she'd got her signals completely crossed.

Marc had already indicated that he definitely wasn't in the market for marriage and, having heard about the devastating end to his first family, she could understand why he'd feel that way.

Until very recently, she'd only been interested in her career and men had just been colleagues. The idea of marriage and a family of her own was a dream she'd given up on long ago, lost with the much-loved dolls and books that had somehow never caught up with her when she'd been taken into care.

It had only been since she'd moved to Edenthwaite and begun working at Denison Memorial that her feelings had slowly begun to change, the friendly atmosphere at work and the stunning surroundings working a subtle magic on her daily life. Those changes had been positively meteoric once she'd realised she could begin to let her guard down with Marc.

Was it possible that his feelings might change, too? If she wasn't much mistaken, he'd already begun to rethink his hasty decision about his career. With time, would he also come to realise that it hadn't been his fault that his wife had tried to drive when she'd been too angry to think clearly? She'd probably never dreamed that her cavalier attitude would cost her and her daughter their lives.

Lauren suddenly realised that she hadn't seen a single picture of his daughter anywhere in Marc's cottage. Had Heather taken after him, with his dark hair and fascinating smoky grey eyes? She could easily imagine her looking like that, her smile a sweeter childish version of his roguish grin.

And as she slowly drifted towards sleep it was only a short step from that mental image to one of a little boy—a perfect miniature of his father and cradled safely in *her* arms.

CHAPTER TEN

THANK goodness for routine, Lauren thought the following afternoon as she hung her coat in her locker and straightened her uniform tunic ready for the start of her shift.

At least if she was at work she'd have plenty to occupy her mind. This morning, she'd nearly gone mad with so much time on her hands and a brain filled with too many questions and not enough answers.

Unfortunately, the way Marc had withdrawn from her last night had made it only too clear that, in spite of the momentary desire she was sure she'd seen in his eyes, he didn't feel the same way about her as she felt about him.

That was *one* question about which she was in no doubt—her feelings about Denison Memorial's senior administrator, Dr Marcus Fletcher.

It might have taken her a dozen years for her emotions to catch up with those of her contemporaries, but since she'd met him she'd slowly come to realise that she'd fallen in love with him—for all the good it would do her if he decided to leave Edenthwaite to resume his medical career. She certainly couldn't go chasing off after him.

'What can't be cured must be endured,' she reminded herself briskly then added her own rider—the one she'd decided on all those years ago when she'd promised herself she'd never be a victim again— 'Unless you can throw it over your shoulder and give it a good kick.'

'Good afternoon, Sonia. Anything interesting happen while I was away?' she asked as she joined her opposite number.

'What *hasn't* been happening?' Sonia exclaimed, obviously eager to bring Lauren up to date. 'You've missed quite a bit of excitement while you've had your day off, and it's partly your fault.'

'My fault?' Lauren cringed inside, wondering if her distraction over her upcoming outing with Marc had caused her to forget something major.

Or was it something to do with that wretched Robert Wainwright again? This was beginning to feel like common or garden harassment. If he didn't stop his campaign soon, perhaps she ought to have a word with someone about a restraining order.

She was still wondering if she had the phone number of the policeman who'd been dealing with Wainwright's various allegations when she realised Sonia was talking nineteen to the dozen and she hadn't heard a word.

Rather than ask her to begin again and open herself up to all sorts of questions about her lack of attention, she kept quiet and tried to work out what had been said at the beginning of the tale.

'Anyway, then the rugby player laughed and said that no girl would ever get the better of him and he could prove it. And then, right in front of a bar full of people, he grabbed hold of a handful of Sam's hair in one hand and—'

'Sam?' Lauren gasped. 'From my classes?'

'Yes! That's what I've been telling you,' Sonia said impatiently. 'A friend of Sam's has been going out with the lout and because of his temper was too afraid to tell him she wanted to end it. Sam was telling her about your classes and he overheard.'

Lauren felt sick. Sam was intelligent and she'd picked up the lessons very quickly, but she'd only started three weeks ago. She shouldn't have had to face a bully like that.

'What happened?' she asked, dreading the answer.

'Sam had to spend the night with us, but the rugby player's friends will never let him live it down.'

'But what *happened*?' Lauren repeated, for once completely out of patience with Sonia's love of spinning a yarn out. Sam had been injured, and if she herself was partly to blame...

'All right! I'm getting there!' Sonia said huffily. 'According to Sam's friend—she works in A and E, too—her boyfriend—now definitely her *ex*-boyfriend—grabbed Sam's hair, said something like, "Get out of that, then," and stood there grinning around at his friends.'

'And?' Lauren prompted, coming close to shaking the woman for taking so long.

'Well, apparently Sam just grabbed hold of his hand and flung him over her shoulder with a crash, even though he weighs *twice* as much as she does!'

'So what went wrong? Why did *she* end up coming in for observation?'

'Well, apparently when the great ox went down he upset a table of drinks and when Sam turned round to walk away she slipped and fell, nearly knocking herself out on the edge of the next table.'

Lauren's relief was profound. She'd been so worried that Sam might have got herself into an impossible situation just because she was over-confident.

'Is she all right now?' She glanced around the ward but couldn't see any sign of the bubbly young woman from where she was.

'She went home at about eleven this morning, escorted like a conquering hero,' Sonia reported with a broad grin. 'And the best thing is, the rugby lout has apparently decided to shake the dust of Edenthwaite from his boots and accept a transfer to another branch of the firm he works for.'

'Well, hooray for that,' Lauren agreed, knowing that the man had lost so much face that Sam might have been at risk of a reprisal attack if he'd stayed. And as bullies weren't very likely to play fair, she could have been badly hurt if he'd wanted revenge at any price.

'Any other excitement?' she asked, hoping that everything else would be blissfully average.

'Well, there's a message for you to contact that gorgeous Marc Fletcher as soon as you get here,' Sonia reported pointedly. 'Have you managed the impossible and actually got him to notice something other than his paperwork?' There was an unmistakable look in her eyes that told Lauren she was avid for gossip.

'It probably *is* paperwork he's interested in,' she said, not allowing herself to hope that there might be a more personal element to the request. And she certainly wouldn't mention the ongoing situation with Robert Wainwright to an inveterate tattle-tale like Sonia. 'As I've been teaching Sam in the self-defence classes, he'll probably need a statement from me for the police.'

'Oh, is that all?' Sonia pulled a disappointed face then perked up again at a sudden thought. 'If you need me to stay on for a bit while you go and see him, a bit of overtime pay wouldn't go amiss. Christmas is getting closer every day.'

Lauren laughed at the heavy hint. 'I'd better phone him to find out, then.'

Sonia was long gone by the time Marc arrived on the ward for the meeting they'd arranged and, in spite of the fact he was in an ordinary suit, there was no mistaking the man following him for anything other than a policeman.

Neither could Lauren stop her eyes from zeroing in on the slim folder he carried under one arm, knowing what it contained.

'Come into the office,' she invited, hoping her voice didn't betray the nerves that had been building up over the last hour and a half. 'I can offer you a choice of tea or coffee, neither of them in a plastic cup or from a machine.'

It seemed to take for ever before they were settled with their steaming cups. Lauren had subconsciously barricaded herself behind the safety of her desk while the detective had taken one of the visitors' chairs, but Marc had surprised her by leaning against the filing cabinet beside her, almost protectively close to her.

The thought that he was concerned about her was like balm to her soul after last night, but she was almost ready to scream with tension by the time her visitor cleared his throat and flipped open the cover of the folder.

'We don't usually do enquiries of this nature,' he said by way of a preface. 'If someone's interested in tracing their family there are other routes, but in your case, with criminal allegations being made about you, we needed to verify your identity without any possibility of doubt.'

'She knows all that,' Marc growled impatiently, and out of the corner of her eye Lauren saw him shift from one foot to the other as though he was itching to take charge. 'Don't drag it out, man. Can't you see the state she's in?'

'Sorry about that, but I'm rather used to following procedure,' he apologised with a grimace.

'You hereby have permission to get straight to the point,' Marc said swiftly, and was sent a wry look for his pains.

'Well, Miss Scott,' the police officer began, and Lauren interrupted.

'Please, can you call me Lauren? It seems less...' She shrugged, at a loss for the word she wanted.

'All right, then. Lauren.' He sent her a wide smile that would probably have knocked the socks off most women, but Lauren couldn't have been less interested. 'With the information you gave us, we were able to go back along the paper trail to confirm that you were adopted at birth. Then we hit a bit of a brick wall because, as you'd told us, your adoption was privately arranged. It seems that someone had gone to a great deal of trouble to try to hide the identity of the natural mother.'

He glanced down at the open file and picked up a piece of paper that he held out towards Lauren.

'It was only when we checked the original register of your birth that we realised there were *two* babies registered at the same time and the information that they'd been born nine minutes apart. If you look at the column for the date, you'll see the figures for the actual time of your birth. That should always be put on record when there is a multiple birth.'

'So I *am* a twin,' Lauren breathed, delight warring with disappointment that she'd had to wait twenty-eight years to find out. 'And my sister...?'

'As you've probably guessed, she's this Laurel Wainwright.'

'Daughter of the overbearing Robert,' Marc muttered under his breath, but Lauren heard him clearly and hid her smile. Suddenly she couldn't be as angry with the man since it was due to his determination to track his daughter down that Lauren had made this momentous discovery.

But that didn't tell her why he would have decided to keep one daughter and not the other, unless...

'Is she adopted, too?' she demanded eagerly, feeling an immediate kinship.

'I'm afraid I haven't looked into her information other than to verify that you were twins. I was more interested in getting together enough proof about your identity to stop Mr Wainwright attacking your reputation and sending people to harass you into "returning home".'

Lauren flopped back in her chair with all the elegance of a puppet with its strings cut, suddenly completely drained of energy by the activity going on inside her head.

'So, I'm *not* alone any more,' she said softly, glancing up instinctively to meet Marc's equally delighted smile as the wonderful news spread through her like sunshine.

On impulse, she held her hand out towards him and when he didn't immediately take it she wondered if she'd made an embarrassing *faux pas*. Then his smile widened and he took the single step that brought him to her side, his hand enclosing hers with warmth and acceptance.

'I suppose that now I know he's my father, I'll have to decide whether to meet this Robert Wainwright,' she said with a shiver of discomfort. She would far rather concentrate on Marc's apparent change of mood.

'You'd be able to ask why he kept one daughter and had the other adopted,' their forgotten audience added, dragging Lauren out of her preoccupation. 'I can't understand how anyone could *think* of separating twins like that. It's such a magical bond.'

'Well, perhaps it won't be too late to form a bond as adults,' Lauren suggested. 'All I have to do now is find a way of meeting her, since she still seems to be missing.'

Before the detective could comment there was the sound of raised voices outside, apparently coming from somewhere near the entrance to the ward.

Lauren recognised the perennially calm tones of her staff nurse but the man's voice was unfamiliar. Given the fact that it was getting closer, that wouldn't be the case for long.

The blinds covering the wide glass panels that made up one whole wall of her office were tilted open so she had a clear view of the heavily built, florid-faced man who rapped on the door, his pale blue eyes boring angrily into hers through the glass.

Without waiting for an invitation he opened it and stepped in.

'There you are at last!' he exclaimed, his fists planted belligerently on his hips. 'It's about time this nonsense came to an end, my girl. I've got a business to run and you're just wasting time. Pack your things and come home with me now and I'll drop the charges over the car.'

'Robert Wainwright?' Lauren asked hesitantly as she slowly straightened to her feet. She wasn't certain what she felt about confronting the cause of all her troubles since she'd come to Edenthwaite without a bit of time to prepare herself. She did know that she didn't like the man very much—far too domineering. Was that why her sister had left home?

'You can stop that playacting for a start,' he snorted. 'You wouldn't have caused me half this trouble if you'd just taken your medication when you were given—'

'If you wouldn't mind keeping your voice down, there are sick people out there,' Marc broke in with a pointed gesture towards the ward.

Lauren could tell from the tension in the supportive hand he'd placed at her waist that he didn't like the man any more than she did. And he was her father?

'Are you Robert Wainwright?' Marc demanded, although there seemed little doubt.

'And what's it to you if I am?' the man blustered. 'This is between my daughter and me.'

'It might be if she were your daughter,' interrupted the detective succinctly.

'And who are *you*?' the big man demanded, rounding on him.

'Just the police inspector who's been investigating your false accusations against a totally innocent young woman,' he replied mildly.

'False accusations! Rubbish! Every one of them is true! She's my daughter, Laurel, she disappeared with my car and now she's calling herself Lauren Scott and claiming to be a nurse. If you knew where she's been hiding out, why haven't you arrested her yet...or have you come to do that now?'

'There won't be *any* arrest because this young lady is exactly who she says she is. Her name is Lauren Scott and she's a fully qualified ward sister properly employed at Denison Memorial hospital. *And*,' he continued when Wainwright tried to interrupt, 'she has all the documents to prove it and they've all been verified by police investigators.'

'That's a complete load of bull,' Robert Wainwright said rudely. 'I sent you my daughter's picture. Any fool can see that's her. All she's done is had her hair cut.' He turned to rant at Lauren directly. 'It'll take more than a few minutes with a pair of scissors to hide who you are, so you might as well give up the pretence right now.'

'Sir,' the detective interrupted before Lauren had a chance to say a word. 'If you wouldn't mind having a look at a couple of pieces of paper before you say any more.'

He handed the man one piece of paper from his folder and when he reached for the copy of her birth certificate from the desk, Lauren thought he'd found the quickest way to convince the man of the truth.

'What does this mean?' Wainwright demanded, looking from one to the other with a thunderous frown. 'They're identical except someone made a mistake when they copied her name onto the second one. It's Laurel.' He stressed the final letter as he held the papers out towards the inspector dismissively.

'Look again, sir,' he said politely. 'You'll see that

these are copies of the original entries in the register and bear consecutive identification numbers. If you look at the column for the date of birth you'll find the notation for the time of birth that tells you Lauren and Laurel are twins.'

'*Twins?*' he scorned. 'That's impossible. She wouldn't have dared hide the fact that she was having…' He suddenly clamped his mouth shut as though aware that he might be giving away more than was wise. His face was noticeably paler when he changed tack. 'So where *is* my daughter, then? Where's Laurel Wainwright?'

'I'm afraid I couldn't possibly tell you, sir. You informed us that Miss Scott was an impostor and a thief so we were investigating *her*. As she's obviously neither of those things we won't need to bother her any further.'

'But…' he began to bluster again, only to be ignored.

'On the other hand,' the detective continued brusquely as he stood and crossed the little room to the door, 'my files will be going to my superior officer who will have to make a decision as to whether there will be charges made against you for wasting police time, harassing a member of the public and defamation of character. In fact, it would be a very good idea if you were to come down to the police station straight away so we can get the matter sorted out.'

He held the door open in an obvious invitation for Robert Wainwright to precede him out of it.

He'd actually taken the first steps to complying when Lauren found her voice.

'Just a minute,' she called hesitantly. 'If Laurel's

your daughter, doesn't that mean you're my father, too?'

'Certainly not,' he snapped. 'My wife and I adopted her just after she was born.' And with that he strode out of the room.

At the last moment, and out of Robert Wainwright's sight, the detective slipped a single sheet of paper out of the file and slid it surreptitiously on top of the nearest stack of paperwork with a pointed glance before shutting the door behind him.

Marc immediately stepped across to collect it.

'What is it?' Lauren demanded impatiently, but he didn't even glance at it as he handed it to her, apparently content to allow her the privilege of reading it first.

At first she wasn't certain what she was reading. She'd been through so many emotions in the last few hours that her brain was overloaded. Finally, it dawned on her that she was looking at a brief résumé of the detective's findings.

The last item on the sheet was a hastily scribbled addition and Lauren had a sudden mental image of the detective writing something in the file at some stage during one of Robert Wainwright's tirades.

Hope swelled so quickly that she was almost afraid to speak. Could this be her twin's address? 'Look, Marc. Do you think…?' She held the paper out towards him.

'I definitely think it's worth a trip to find out, and as soon as possible, don't you? But not tonight,' he added quickly. 'You've already got another appointment as soon as you finish work.'

'Have I?' She blinked, trying to remember what she had planned.

'With me?' he suggested a shade diffidently. 'I've been doing a lot of thinking since we last spoke.'

She'd slowly come to know the far more vulnerable character he hid behind the façade of the decisive man he always appeared to be at the hospital, but she couldn't tell anything from his expression at the moment. That fact alone was enough to make her nervous.

Was he going to tell her that he'd decided to go back to medicine, that he'd be leaving Edenthwaite and her? In a way she really hoped he was, because it was the right thing for him, but her heart would probably never recover from the loss.

There was only one way to find out.

'If everything goes smoothly at the end of my shift I should be home by half past nine,' she offered.

'Perfect,' he agreed. 'I'll see you then.' And without another word, he strode out of her office.

'Stop fussing and sit down!' Marc told himself when he found himself neatening the already perfect cutlery placement for the umpteenth time.

But it was almost impossible to stay still when so much rested on the events of the next couple of hours. How could he have known that his feelings for Lauren would have become so much more than caring?

The quick tap at the door sent his pulse rate into orbit and wasn't nearly enough warning before Lauren stepped into the narrow hallway.

'Am I too early?' she asked as she slipped her coat off. He took it from her.

'No. You're perfect,' he said clumsily, then realised the words were very apt. She *was* perfect...for him. Now all he had to do was persuade her of the fact and ask her if she was willing to try to put down a few roots. If not, he would have to fall back on plan B because, whatever happened, he wouldn't easily let her go. In fact, he had no intention of letting her go at all.

'Mmm, something smells wonderful!' she exclaimed as they reached the kitchen. 'Is there anything I can do to help?'

'Nothing except make yourself comfortable,' he directed, holding out the chair for her. He paused just long enough to breathe in the herbal scent of her shampoo then had to remind himself that he had a meal to serve.

He went to take the dish out of the oven and suddenly realised that in spite of the fact it was his delicious never-fail recipe for chicken in red wine, he wouldn't be able to eat a mouthful of it until he'd spoken to her; until he'd found out whether there was a chance...

He stood again and turned to face her.

'Lauren, I've been thinking about what you said,' he burst out suddenly, unable to wait any longer.

'About what?' She blinked up at him, looking startled and a little apprehensive. Was she picking up on his tension?

'About the fact that I'd be far happier as a doctor than a paper-pusher,' he said bluntly as he pulled his own chair out from the table and turned it to face her before he sank onto it. 'You were right, of course, and once I'd admitted that, a whole lot of other things just seemed to fall into place in my mind.'

'What sort of things?' she asked, and he was uncomfortably aware that she didn't seem nearly as pleased as he'd been expecting. Had he read everything wrong? Well, it was too late to stop now.

'Things like looking for a doctor's job in the Edenthwaite area, preferably one based at Denison Memorial. Then advertising my admin post and interviewing my replacement. Then contacting an architect to have him draw up plans for converting these two cottages into one...'

Marc realised he was saying too much when he had to stop to draw in a much-needed breath, and he hadn't said the most important thing at all yet.

He leaned forward to take her hands in his.

'But most of all,' he continued softly, aware that his feelings were probably written all over his face but unable to care at that moment, 'most of all, I realised that I'll never be happy anywhere unless I'm with you.'

He held his breath while he waited for her to say something, anything, and then her eyes filled with tears.

'Lauren! What's the matter?'

His heart sank like a stone. The last thing he'd wanted had been to upset her.

'Please, don't cry, sweetheart. I know we haven't known each other very long and anyone would have reservations about marrying an old crock like me, and I know it's too soon for you to be certain, but I just couldn't wait to—'

'Marc?' she said softly, stopping his frantic babbling with a gentle finger on his mouth. 'Are you ever going to stop talking long enough to kiss me, or are you waiting for written permission?'

With a wordless whoop of delight he swept her out of her chair and swung her round, but there wasn't really enough room for that sort of celebration in such a tiny kitchen.

'You *will* marry me?' he demanded as he carried her swiftly through to the sitting room, automatically making for the cosy spot in front of the glowing fire that was already part of their shared memories. If he had his way, the two of them were going to spend a lot more time just here in the future.

'Of course I'll marry you,' she said, her eyes shining at him through her tears. 'I was so afraid when you said you were going to go back to being a doctor. I knew you'd made the right decision but I thought I was going to lose you.'

He smoothed the moisture from her cheeks, amazed that she was actually crying because she was happy. It was going to take a lifetime to unravel her complexities.

'I couldn't go away if you were here. It would be like tearing my heart out,' he said, then broached his only remaining serious concern. 'Lauren, we both know how much you've moved around since you qualified. Do you feel you could put down roots here or will you always have itchy feet?'

'It might not look like it on my CV, but I've never had itchy feet. I only ever moved because I never found what I was looking for—a place that felt like home.'

'And does Edenthwaite feel like home?' he asked as he gave in to the urge to lift her onto his lap. For the first time he could savour the feel of her in his arms, knowing that it was the start of a lifetime together.

'It will be home with you here,' she said happily, wrapping her arms around him and turning her face up to him. 'I didn't know what I was looking for, but I've found what I've always wanted—a love of my own.'

'And children?' he suggested, suddenly knowing that, even though he'd lost Heather, there was enough love inside him now for a whole tribe, if that was what Lauren wanted.

She hardly needed to say anything. Her smile said it all.

'Lots of children,' she corrected, to his silent amusement. How had he guessed? 'After all, we've got the whole of Cumbria as their playground so they'll never run out of space.'

'And one day we'll go and find your sister, too,' he promised. 'It might not be in time for the wedding, because I don't intend waiting very long.'

'Well, then,' she said thoughtfully, apparently unaware of the wicked gleam that had appeared in her eyes, 'that just leaves me with one question.'

'And that is?' Desire had already started to coil inside him.

'Well, I gave you permission to kiss me ages ago and nothing happened. Do ex-soldiers only respond to direct orders?'

Her whisky-coloured eyes were filled with newly awakened need and Marc cradled her face between his hands and marvelled that she'd given her heart to him.

'Lauren, you won't need to give me orders and I'm definitely not the sort to wait to be given permission. Now that you've told me you love me, all you have to do is ask.'

'Really?' she said, with the first hint of coquetry he'd ever heard from her, and his body responded in an instant. 'In that case, how about taking me up to your bedroom? There are a few things I need to learn if we're going to be a family, and you're the perfect man to teach me.'

Modern Romance™
...seduction and
passion guaranteed

Tender Romance™
...love affairs that
last a lifetime

Sensual Romance™
...sassy, sexy and
seductive

Blaze
...sultry days and
steamy nights

Medical Romance™
...medical drama on
the pulse

Historical Romance™
...rich, vivid and
passionate

27 new titles every month.

*With all kinds of Romance for
every kind of mood...*

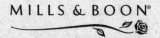

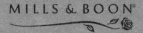

MILLS & BOON®

Medical Romance™

CHRISTMAS KNIGHT by Meredith Webber

As the only doctor in Testament – and a mother with a tiny baby – Kate was floundering until a knight in shining leathers drove up to her door. Local bad boy Grant Bell was now a doctor and he'd come to help. He was wonderful with Kate's patients, and with her baby – but Grant had a fiancée back in Sydney…

A MOTHER FOR HIS CHILD by Lilian Darcy

It had started as one night of passion – and since Will Braggett had become a partner in Maggie's medical practice it had turned into a steamy affair. As a single dad, Will's priority was his son. He wasn't ready to find him a new mother just yet. But Maggie wasn't satisfied simply being his mistress – she insisted they could only have a future if Will allowed her to get to know his child too…

THE IRRESISTIBLE DOCTOR by Carol Wood

Dr Alex Trent loves her new job as GP in a busy country practice. But combining motherhood and a busy career is a challenge, and Alex has no room for a man in her life – until Dr Daniel Hayward explodes onto the scene! Nine years ago their intense relationship collapsed – now Daniel's greatest desire is to reclaim Alex – this time as his wife!

On sale 1st November 2002

Available at most branches of WH Smith, Tesco, Martins, Borders, Eason, Sainsbury's and all good paperback bookshops. 1002/03a

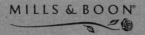

MILLS & BOON

Winter
weddings

Three brand new Christmas novels

Penny Jordan   Gail Whitiker   Judy Christenberry

Published 18th October 2002

*Available at most branches of WH Smith,
Tesco, Martins, Borders, Eason, Sainsbury's
and all good paperback bookshops.*

1102/59/SH39

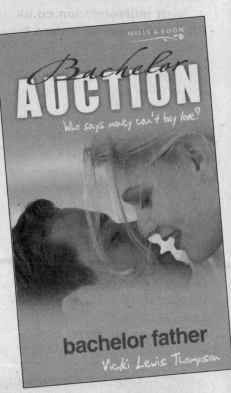

2 FREE

books and a surprise gift!

We would like to take this opportunity to thank you for reading this Mills & Boon® book by offering you the chance to take TWO more specially selected titles from the Medical Romance™ series absolutely FREE! We're also making this offer to introduce you to the benefits of the Reader Service™—

★ FREE home delivery
★ FREE gifts and competitions
★ FREE monthly Newsletter
★ Exclusive Reader Service discount
★ Books available before they're in the shops

Accepting these FREE books and gift places you under no obligation to buy, you may cancel at any time, even after receiving your free shipment. Simply complete your details below and return the entire page to the address below. *You don't even need a stamp!*

YES! Please send me 2 free Medical Romance books and a surprise gift. I understand that unless you hear from me, I will receive 4 superb new titles every month for just £2.55 each, postage and packing free. I am under no obligation to purchase any books and may cancel my subscription at any time. The free books and gift will be mine to keep in any case.

M2ZEA

Ms/Mrs/Miss/Mr ....Initials...................................
BLOCK CAPITALS PLEASE

Surname ....

Address ....

....

....Postcode................................

Send this whole page to:
UK: FREEPOST CN81, Croydon, CR9 3WZ
EIRE: PO Box 4546, Kilcock, County Kildare (stamp required)